# The Reanimation
# of Robert

Erin Ritch

No Wyverns Publishing
PO Box 32
Dorena, OR 97434
NoWyverns.com

Cover Illustration by Char Houweling
HouwelingDesign.com

ISBN: 9781790595
ISBN-13: 9781790595594

# DEDICATION

To my loving husband Nick, it would take a full-length novel
to express how grateful I am for all your support whether it be
emotionally, creatively, or technically. Many people play a part
in encouraging my career, including my precious grandparents
who both passed away while writing this book. I thank them as
well, for showing me that a life lived right has nothing to fear
from death.

# ACKNOWLEDGMENTS

I would like to sincerely thank Kat McCartney, Harley David Tomlinson, and Brian Ross for generously sharing their time and likeness as subjects for Piper, Alex, and Robert on the cover of this book. You did a fantastic job and I truly appreciate you helping out. Another special thanks to Cindy Wormsbecker, my trusted Beta reader and friend who shares insightful (and always tactful) critique and feedback on my stories. You are a true gem, thank you for believing in me and being a part of the process.

# CONTENTS

# 1 DAY DEAD

"If you had the chance to change it all, would you?" Death asked.

He stared into the void. The man could hear the voice, feel the vibration as the sound waves rumbled beneath his feet, a rising storm that washed over him with command. But no matter how hard he looked and searched, he could not see through the thick darkness all around him. A coldness defiled the layers of his skin, seeping through and leaving old flesh behind, right there in that dark place between the living and the dead.

A spotlight appeared, blinding to the man's eyes. He shielded himself from the light until his eyes adjusted and a form began to take shape. It was a woman's limp body suspended midair, her hair falling back from her head like a frail waterfall. He would have recognized that hair anywhere, for years he fell asleep to its soft scent, splayed across the pillowcase beside him.

"For her?" He finally found his voice. He wanted to run to her but she appeared lost in a dream, unaware of this place and this darkness.

"Yes, for her," Death confirmed.

"What do I do? What do you want?"

"I will need your service. I will need your utter devotion for anything I ask."

The illumination on the woman began to slowly dim.

"Yes!" the man shouted. He tried to move his legs but he had no control, crumbling to the ground instead. "Yes! I said, yes! Anything!" he shouted again with the last remains of his voice.

"Then I will keep her here," Death said, raising the woman closer and closer to the source of the light until she was out of sight. "Asleep, for now."

The spotlight pivoted with a snap and targeted the man. He cried out at the intense heat, his gray skin crackling and burning pink then red. He stood and clawed at himself, itching with raging blood. He heard his voice in his head, roaring and screaming back to life. Above him, the woman twirled in a limp pirouette, her hand dangling further and further beyond his reach.

"Answer my call," Death said, the voice trailing into a whisper. The spotlight grew brighter and brighter until it flooded every corner of the darkness. "Or she remains mine."

# 156 DAYS DEAD

"Robert?"

He stared out the front window at the dead cat across the street. The animal had been there yesterday and the day before. It was Monday when Robert first saw it and he had thought to himself, *What a way to start the work week*. To walk down the street and see the smashed skull of an innocent animal, left to deteriorate in the sewer drain. Maybe it was intentionally left there, maybe not. Another nameless victim caught on that congested street, the same busy street that forced Robert to walk to work instead of drive.

"Robert. Soy latte for Robert."

He felt his eyes start to glaze over as he stared through the blur of traffic towards the lifeless figure on the ground. Dozens of people passed by with their noses buried in their phones, completely oblivious yet still able to navigate the swirling crowds. Robert blinked. *Seattle*. This city with its busy streets and overpriced rent, and now, sewer drains of dead cats.

A hand reached over and gently tapped his shoulder. "Robert. Your soy latte."

One of the baristas, Piper, stood before him. She was holding his soy latte carefully cradled in her hands. Extra hot just as he always asked for it, he could tell by the steam twisting through the vent on the lid. But Piper knew that already. He had been coming to Avenue Coffee every weekday for years. He had been there when it was Piper's first day, her red hair stuck to her small and sweaty face, her speech flustered and rushed as she stumbled over her orders and dropped an entire jug of milk. But he had asked for his soy latte extra hot and she had delivered it perfectly. His wife had always ordered the special-of-the-day because her tastes could change on a whim. Claire had been like that, slightly different every day. Sometimes he thought Piper kept up with her better than he had.

"I didn't hear you," Robert stumbled, taking the cup from her.

Piper smiled as she wiped her hands on her dingy black apron. "I know." She followed his line of sight out the window. It was raining that morning, as usual. "What?"

Robert glanced down at her quickly. He liked looking at her face, void of wrinkles and age, more than he liked to admit. He took a sip of his latte and nodded towards the window. "There's a dead cat out there. Been there for days."

Piper scowled. "Ugh, sad." She shrugged her shoulders. "I'm sure someone will take care of it."

He took another long sip of his latte. "Eventually."

Piper looked over her shoulder at the line of people at the counter. Her coworker raised her hands in a show of exasperation. "Gotta go. See you tomorrow."

Robert nodded and mumbled some form of thank you. He pulled out his phone to check the time. He had to hurry if he was going to get to work on time. As he pushed his way towards the door, Robert caught a glimpse of himself in the front window's reflection. He saw a man in his late thirties, maybe even early forties as evidenced from the streaks of gray in his dark brown hair. A tall man, too thin as though malnourished, which only made him look even older. His skin appeared shockingly pale and Robert hoped that was simply an effect of the reflection. His bulky, faded jacket was old as well. It had been a gift from Claire years ago. She had threatened that this Christmas would be the one where she finally replaced it. But that wasn't going to happen, anymore.

The bell hanging on the door rang shrilly and Robert was outside once again. Like a blast to the face, the sounds and smells and noises of the city seared him like a nuclear wind. His only source of comfort was that steaming soy latte grasped with all his might on that cold November morning. It was his beacon, his light that distracted him from the darkness. He focused on that cup. Just him and the steam, floating down the street until they both evaporated into thin air.

That evening, Robert decided to take another route home from work. Typically, he walked the way of Avenue Coffee in the morning and then an alternate path on the way home. This path took him by what Claire used to call *happy windows*. When the small remainder of day encouraged people to leave their window curtains open, allowing the opportunity to have a quick glimpse of their lives, reunited after a long day at work or school or life. And lately, more than ever, Robert lived for those happy glimpses. But in the bare light of that evening sky, he broke from routine and walked back towards Avenue Coffee.

The city felt strange, like an alien place that he was somewhat familiar with but right then, in that fading light, may as well have been the surface of the moon. Avenue Coffee was closed up, the tables cleared with the chairs stacked atop them, chained for good measure. With a break in traffic, Robert lumbered across the street and knelt down at the storm drain. As the last thread of evening illumination trailed away, the street light over the sidewalk flickered to life.

The cat was still there and in fact, it was a kitten. Robert's first reaction was to recoil. The battered remains of the small animal were a distorted mess of matted orange and white fur and broken bones. The corpse was covered in ants and other mites. And then there was the odor of death. Robert would recognize it anywhere. He had first encountered it that day in the morgue, Claire's expressionless face staring at the ceiling above the coroner's table. It was a stench from another world, a scent that could not be masked, no matter how many chemicals you tried to drown it out with. Robert touched the animal's tiny paw and felt the unmistakable absence of life.

Searching through his jacket pockets, Robert withdrew his discarded paper lunch sack and unfolded it. Carefully nudging the remains of the animal with the edge of his sleeve, Robert scooped the kitten into the paper bag and neatly folded it closed. It disturbed him how light the bag was, a paper sack of old life. It should have been squirming and heavy with pulsing blood. He carried it reverently down the street until he reached his house.

He and Claire had purchased their house when they were young and broke. Having both grew up in apartments, they dreamed of buying a home where they didn't share a wall with a neighbor. They would walk the streets and fantasize about which house was right for them. That one was too big. That one was too small. Then one day, they took a wrong street and stumbled upon a floating house. Or so they thought in that evening hour when the lanterns on the nearby docks reflected off each other, making the house appear to hover on a sea of light. When they returned the next morning, to that house of brick and mortar on the banks of the rocking docks, they knew it was still the home of their dreams.

They could by no means afford it; she was a teacher's assistant, he was a laborer at the pier. How they had been approved for a loan, Robert never understood. He remembered nights on the hardwood floors, those creaky boards settling beneath his back as though attempting to form to the curve of his spine. He and Claire had laughed at their poorness and zipped their sleeping bags together for extra warmth. It took them months to save up for a couch and even longer for a television. But even then, they would still spend their evenings in the laundry room, silently watching the sunset out the little window that captured the best view, every time, every night.

Robert unlocked the front door and slowly shut it behind him. He didn't want to drop the bag and cause more damage than had already been done. He hadn't thought past this moment. He had hoped if he got home, he would be offering some small bit of safety to this dead animal, the same feeling of security that he felt in this place. He placed the bag on the kitchen table as the sound of scuttling toenails scratched through the house. Jasper, his Jack Russell Terrier, came bounding around the hallway corner and sliding into the kitchen. He offered Robert a quick greeting before immediately jumping up against the table and howling.

"Shush, Jasper, boy! Down!" Robert picked up the small animal. He had purchased that wriggling bundle of energy for Claire on the one-month anniversary of their first miscarriage. Meant as a distraction, Jasper would become a sort of substitute for the child they lost and the two afterwards. A small and warm body in the dark, cold bed. A source of comfort without having to utter a single word. Or as Claire called him, her life preserver in a sea of thoughts.

Robert put Jasper outside. They had a small backyard, outfitted very basically for Jasper so that he could relieve himself without having to be walked on a leash. It was a luxury many of their city friends didn't have, the ones who lamented about having to put on their coat and boots to take their dog out for a 3 am piss. Preparing Jasper's dinner, he let the dog back inside and snuck outside with the kitten bag.

Since losing his wife, Robert had acquired a new respect for life. And in that same way, death. He expected this was all part of his grieving process. Before Claire's death, he had no issue swatting a fly with his morning newspaper and finding triumph in its demise. But now he was using that morning newspaper to guide the fly outside to greener pastures. He was waiting until the spider in the shower was safely out of the way before turning on the water. He even ignored the mouse that had taken up residence in his kitchen cupboards, although Jasper had a difficult time embracing the same outlook.

Robert could not simply dump the kitten's body in the waterway or a trash can. Both would have been suitable for an animal with no connection to him, but not for Robert in his current state of mind. Rummaging through the patio closet until he found his shovel, Robert walked around to the side of the house where the electric meter stood. The ground there was unkempt and mossy, safe from Jasper's prying paws. In the faint light provided by the kitchen window, Robert dug a shallow hole and placed the paper bag inside. He paused before covering it again with dirt. He thought, after all it had gone through, the kitten at least deserved a pause.

Robert returned inside and he and Jasper watched television as they did, night after night. After an hour, Robert sent Japer up to bed as he turned off the lights around the house. He stopped and peered outside the kitchen window at the small grave. The fresh dirt looked richly black beside the fuzzy, dull moss. Robert turned the exterior light back on and shuffled to bed. He thought, after all it had gone through, the kitten at least deserved a light in the darkness.

# 170 DAYS DEAD

"Robert?"

Piper waited at the counter, the steaming soy latte sweltering against her hand. Extra hot, as always requested. She usually had about a 50/50 chance that he would hear her. He was the most distracted man she had ever met. Every morning it was as though that was his first visit to Avenue Coffee, clearly specifying time after time that the drink should be extra hot and soy, always soy. She had known this man, in a way, for years now. Yet still, he reminded her that his name was Robert.

"Soy latte for Robert!" she called again, louder. Piper glanced over at her manager, who was shaking his head. He threw up his hands and walked away.

"This guy!" Piper's co-worker, Zelda, whispered sharply. She raised the corners of her red lips into a hint of a snarl. "Every time!"

"Not *every* time," Piper corrected. She cleared her throat in preparation for another attempt to secure Robert's attention.

But Robert was staring out the window, lost. Piper imagined his mind must be a place of a thousand doorways and he was on task to open them all. Maybe one day he would find what he was looking for. The last thing he had time to do was listen if his soy latte was ready. She felt a pang of sympathy for the poor guy. His wife's murder had rattled their little corner of Seattle barely five months ago, when Claire's lifeless body was discovered in an alleyway outside her school. Piper remembered the woman and her delicate hands, always tipping in change. No one tipped in change, anymore.

Although Robert had been cleared of suspicion for Claire's killing, there were too many that still suspected the quiet man who grew even more reserved as the weeks and months progressed. Piper had hidden the newspapers from the tables for weeks when Robert finally began to return. Buried within his jacket, he would lumber up to the counter, a strange remnant of the man he was before.

"Robert!" a deep voice boomed across the coffee shop. The air filled with snickers as a dozen faces looked up from their phones, books, or computers. Robert jumped and looked over the sea of tables towards the source of the voice, a man sitting in the far corner, looking very pleased with himself. Robert met the man's gaze and they remained locked there for several beats until he finally turned away.

"Sorry," Robert mumbled to Piper, bowing his head as he reached out to carefully take the soy latte. It was then that he realized he still had dirt under his fingernails from the previous night's burial. "Thanks," he called as he pushed his way through the crowd towards the exit.

Once Robert was outside, Piper turned to Zelda. "I'm going to clean tables," she announced, storming past the next patron.

"What?" Zelda gasped. "They don't need it!"

The man in the corner saw Piper stomping towards him, causing him to sit up straight and quickly remove his feet from the chair next to him. His dark brown hair was neatly combed into place and secured there with a generous amount of gel. He was dressed sharply in a well-tailored pair of khakis and button down with a vest. The man appeared done with his coffee, a stack of folders and notes on the table beside him. The corners of his eyes crinkled as he smiled at Piper's approach.

"Sir," Piper snapped, seizing the empty coffee cup. "Please don't interfere with my job in the future." She leaned in a bit closer. "It's rude."

The man's face was frozen in masked amusement. Finally, he let out a long sigh and shrugged. "I apologize. But I know the man and he can be a bit, let's say, absentminded."

Piper straightened. "You know Robert?"

The man extended his hand. It was well-manicured but looked strong. "I'm Alex Shaw. What's your name?"

Piper pointed to her name tag and raised an eyebrow.

"Piper," Alex read aloud, withdrawing his hand. "Nice to meet you."

"Am I supposed to know who you are?" Piper questioned, her eyebrow still raised.

"Well," Alex laughed loudly, smoothing back his still well-coifed hair. "Not necessarily. Do you know Robert, as well?"

"A bit," Piper answered, still sizing the man up. She had seen him in the coffee shop several times before, usually with his back to the wall at one of the far corner tables. "He's a very nice man, just quiet. His wife was murdered earlier this year, and as usual, the husband is suspected. It's messed up, I think."

"Well," Alex urged, leaning forward. "Did he?"

"What?"

"Kill his wife?"

"No way," Piper insisted, shaking her head. "I don't get that vibe from him."

"The murderer vibe?"

"You know what I mean," Piper said through a smile.

"I do, actually." Alex smiled back. "Guess we have something in common already." He reached into his wallet and pulled out a card. On the creamy stock, the raised gold lettering read *Alexander Shaw, Homicide Detective.*

Piper struggled to keep composed. Now she knew why her gaze was drawn to him. Now she knew why he seemed familiar. She had seen him on the news, knew his name from the newspapers. He was one of the investigators in the case surrounding Robert and Claire. Alex watched Piper's thoughts play out across her face.

"I need to get back," she said quietly, attempting to

return the business card.

Alex waved his hands. "Keep it. Maybe you'll need me one day."

"Right." Piper narrowed her eyes, feigning annoyance as she leaned across the table. "Just don't let me catch you yelling at patrons again, got it?"

Alex leaned forward and lowered his voice. "What would you do to me if I did?"

"Have a good day, Detective," Piper said over her shoulder as she walked away. Her heart was pounding in her chest. A pit formed in her stomach as she imagined Robert walking down the sidewalk, seemingly oblivious to the throngs of people around him, a dreamy iceberg in a sea of hot, busy minds.

---

Robert still could not bring himself to read the newspaper article reporting Claire's murder. Or the dozen or so articles that followed. He couldn't stand the coldness of it. How the loss of someone so beautiful could be summed up in a 750-word column that addressed who, what, when, where, and why.

*Why* had never been answered. Claire had been murdered on a Tuesday evening in the alleyway outside her school. They said there had been a struggle. They said she had fought back. They said she died quickly. But why she had been killed, they did not know. And now, six months later, why was not important, anymore.

*Why* was a question that Robert had become very familiar with. *Why were you not there? Why were you working late? Why was Claire waiting for you? Why didn't you just tell her to go home? Why don't you know who killed her? Why are you alive and she isn't?*

Robert turned on his cell phone. He scrolled back to the text message he looked at each and every morning.

*See u soon, lots to talk about!!!*

That text message brought him the slightest bit of light at the start of each day. He smiled to think of her typing that message, her face beaming as she added exclamation point after exclamation point. It was rushed, very unlike her. And why she was so excited, Robert did not know. It wasn't their walk home, that was an every weeknight occurrence. They were not waiting for any news. No lottery tickets were purchased that he knew of. There were no clues in her purse or coat.

And why he was still alive, Robert did not know. He was supposed to have been in that alleyway too, lying next to Claire in a pile of swirling term papers. Why had he worked late? Robert strained to remember. That night was decaying in his mind, second after second. His memory seemed to be eroding, detail after detail, as though walling himself away from the pain.

"Why," Robert whispered from the laundry room window. He asked no one in particular, except maybe the early morning mists hanging around the pier. Or Jasper, whose snores were audible even from across the house. Closing his eyes, Robert pushed himself to that day, right from the beginning, starting with a misty morning just like the one unfolding before him.

It began with a cup of coffee, as usual. Robert's day always started with one home brewed cup. Bleary-eyed and shuffling towards the coffee machine, he would fill the pot with just enough water to brew two cups of coffee. One for him, one for Claire. She drank it out of habit but Robert needed the liquid courage. His career at the Port of Seattle had never been easy. He started out in a warehouse, youthful and with no experience, loading and unloading freight into a freezer. That's when he had started drinking coffee, to brace himself for the eternal cold that waited for him in the stretch of day. He remembered coming home, night after night, and running hot water over his stiff knuckles until the joints finally began to loosen and give way to raw, pink skin.

Over the years, Robert switched between a variety of dock worker positions, but they only dug him deeper into a career he never really wanted in the first place. They took the inexperienced and spit out the lifers who would never get away. Robert convinced himself he liked the glimpses of ocean, the bustle of the port, the power of the forklift at the command of his hands. But if anyone asked what was his dream career or ideal job position, Robert wouldn't have had an answer. It had been plucked from him by the ocean breeze, carried away along with the dreams of his comrades. It had to be that way, they were the necessary casualties to feed the machine that was the Port of Seattle.

The morning of Claire's death had been a gray day. There had been a hint of spring in the days prior, but not that morning or afternoon or night. The wind had been extremely strong, raging against the railings with frothing waves and threatening to rip the clipboard right out of Robert's hands. The day had dragged, as always. The details were blurry from a bleary history of muddled days. It proved difficult for Robert to provide information to the authorities since each day dripped into the next and the day of Claire's murder had been no exception.

But he did remember her text. He remembered feeling the notification buzz in his coat pocket, vibrating against his heart. Robert was not one to get phone calls or texts so it was a rare occasion to use his phone for anything other than an alarm clock. But this is where his memory begins to fade, no matter how hard Robert tries to hold onto the details. He was standing at the dock's railing, staring at the storm that was inching its way across the sea towards the port, holding tight to his clipboard that the wind threatened to whip away. And then everything slowly fades to darkness like a veil dropping from the sky until the next thing Robert remembers is his phone vibrating again and again and again. Although this time it's not from Claire, but about her.

A few coworkers claimed to have seen Robert at the dock past his scheduled shift, but it was not uncommon for him to work an extra hour or two to wrap up a shipment. Others claimed to have left with him right at the close of shift, sharing a quiet bus ride together. But Robert hadn't logged his extra hours and he never took the bus. He could neither confirm or deny anything other than that impending storm and the pages of his clipboard fluttering to break free.

---

On Sunday, Robert liked to relax in the living room with the newspaper sprawled all around him. Sundays were his day off and he was not used to seeing the afternoon sun in his house. He liked it. He was used to the thin light of dawn as he rushed around the kitchen or the dull glow of sunset as he fed Jasper and thumbed through the mail. This was a side of his house that he did not see very often. And he liked it.

A shadow crossed a beam of sunlight on the carpet, catching Robert's eye. He looked over the edge of the newspaper. A small form lithely pounced across the light, swatting at a smaller creature that he assumed was a fly. For a moment, Robert wondered if he had left Jasper outside but then he heard the congested snores from the other side of the couch.

Carefully saving his place in the newspaper article, Robert rose and shuffled stiffly to the back glass door and peered outside. A small orange and white kitten was bounding around the tiny backyard, chasing after the elusive fly. It meowed periodically, purring as it rubbed up against the side of the house. Robert watched the small animal until it suddenly stopped its campaign against the fly and sat down carefully on the bed of soft grass, staring back at him complacently. It blinked slowly and Robert felt the hairs on the back of his neck begin to stand on edge, one by one.

He jumped as Jasper came roaring towards the back door, his paws slipping on the smooth wood floors. The kitten seemed unfazed as Jasper growled from deep in his throat, his bark now mixed with a whine in an attempt to get Robert to open the door. Leisurely wiping its face, the kitten trotted away and disappeared around the side of the house.

That night, Robert left a small bowl of food outside the back door and turned on the porch light. And in the morning, the food was gone. That next evening, he left out another bowl of food. But this time, the food remained. It stayed there for a week until it became soggy and moldy and Robert finally threw it away.

# 191 DAYS DEAD

Fidgeting with the tattered edges of his last pack of cigarettes, Alex waited outside the doorway of the bar. This was truly his last pack of cigarettes, unlike like the last pack and the one before that. This pack contained one lone cigarette, the remaining survivor in the battle for Alex's lungs. Knowing his dark comrade was with him always was a comfort to Alex, a potential means of easing a long night or providing a way out of a useless conversation. He mumbled as he released the soft paper of the cigarette pack and reached into his pants pockets for a foil gum wrapper, popping a fresh piece into his mouth. With a heavy sigh, Alex straightened his shoulders and leaned back against the exterior of the building, focusing again on the apartment complex across the street.

It was raining, as usual. Alex raised the zipper on his leather jacket as high as it would go and tried to keep his entire body under the protection of the overhang. He hated this Pacific Northwest weather and its inhabitants' attempts to combat the dampness with coffee carts on every corner. It didn't help. Not a bit. He broke his gaze long enough to look up as the streetlight flickered to life, illuminating the rain that fell like the fine mist from a waterfall. The darkness only hastened the cold stiffness in Alex's knees, aching from hours of standing. He paced from one foot to the next, willing himself to stay focused on the building across from him. He knew Robert was in there. And he wasn't moving until Robert moved first.

*Robert Castle.* Alex knew the letters so well he could have come up with a thousand anagrams. He had written the name on reports, emails, press releases, text messages, phone messages, even in the condensation on his morning bathroom's steamed-up mirror. The murder case of Claire Castle was his first assignment after his promotion to homicide. There had been many cases since and there would be many more to come, but none rattled him like that one. No suspect antagonized him like slippery Robert, with his forlorn eyes and sketchy story. He had no real details to offer, no real sense of anything. If Alex had believed him, he would have felt sorry for the guy. Maybe it was the failure of an unsolved case or the general strangeness of Robert, but Alex could not let go of this feeling. The feeling that something wasn't right. And it hadn't let him down yet.

So he chose random nights to watch Robert's home for any strange activity, for anything that piqued that instinct. Usually a man of a seemed routine, it wasn't often that Robert left his home other than for work or the grocery store. But tonight was different. Robert walked with a new gait. He jogged across the street without waiting for the crosswalk sign. He walked for a long time without any break or change in pace, down the side of the freeway and taking strange short cuts that made keeping up with Robert difficult. But if that had been the plan, Alex was not swayed. He'd walk across the world if it meant catching Robert Castle.

The door to the bar opened with a loud blast of holiday music with an electronic twist. Two men staggered out, laughing and talking loudly as they fumbled through their coat pockets. One of the men turned to Alex, who was intently staring past them at the building across the street.

"Hey man, got a smoke?" the intoxicated man asked, unsteadily waving for Alex's attention.

Alex thought about the lone cigarette in his pocket, safe within its silky cardboard cocoon. "Nope, sorry," he replied, his gaze locked in front of him.

The man narrowed his eyes and leaned forward. "How about some gum? You got gum?"

"No."

"You're chewing some right now, man!"

As Alex engaged with the two drunk men, he almost missed Robert's lanky form walking down the shrouded sidewalk across the street, shoulders bent over and hands in his coat pockets. Robert had exited the apartment complex without a sound, even appearing to have missed the attention of the security guard outside, whose distracted face was illuminated by his cell phone screen.

Pushing past the two men, Alex ran in Robert's direction, dodging the oncoming traffic. By the time he reached the other side of the street, a commotion had drawn the attention of the distracted security guard, who went rushing into the building. A siren became discernable in the distance and Alex forced himself to stop, cursing as Robert disappeared around the corner and into the darkness. Alex entered the lobby and encountered a group of frantic tenants, all demanding the security guard's attention at once.

"Detective Alex Shaw, Seattle Homicide," Alex announced to the group. "What's going on here?"

"The guy's dead!" one of the tenants shouted. "The man in 16b, he's dead!"

"I just talked to him, today by the mailboxes. He was going to buy a ham for the holidays!"

"Right out on the hallway floor, I'll never be able to able to unsee it. Horrible!"

Alex looked over his shoulder at the doorway and the streets beyond it. That nagging feeling in his gut returned and was telling him to run, to chase down Robert and drag him back. To search his face for any sort of sign that confirmed his suspicions. But it was too late. Instinctively, he had begun taking notes for his report and directing the overwhelmed security guard.

*Next time.*

---

In his sleep, Robert could hear a faint siren. A call in the dark, circling around and around again as it relentlessly hammered Robert for his attention. His alarm clock had been going off as instructed, only ceasing when Robert's hand reached out and knocked it off the table. Sitting up slowly, Robert cradled his pounding head. He heard the familiar crunch of his jacket and looked down. He was fully dressed, down to his shoes still double tied. Jasper watched him from the floor, furry eyebrows raised in a look of caution.

"What?" Robert asked himself, rubbing his head in attempt to bring back the moments from before sleep. He remembered coming home, exhausted from a long day working a shorthanded shift. Dusting off his jacket, he tried to recall coming to bed fully clothed. But he couldn't. He only remembered numbing exhaustion and then sleep. He looked at the clock. He was late, too late to keep contemplating the night before.

"Guess I'm already dressed," he said to Jasper, who continued to observe him from the floor. Once Robert walked past him to the bathroom, Jasper jumped on the bed to his usual sleeping spot, listening to his master with one ear perked to attention.

Splashing cold water on his face, Robert tried to rub the throbbing away. He focused his eyes on the pooling water slowly trickling down the drain, observing faint veins of pink and red. He stood up straight, pawing at the cold water. It was then that he noticed blood beneath his fingertips, heavily caked in some spots.

"What?" Robert asked himself again. Alarm began to flutter in his chest. He examined his hands for wounds but found nothing. He closed his eyes and forced himself back through every moment from the day before. Morning. Breakfast. Coffee. Coffee shop. Walk to work. Work. Work. Clock out. Walk home. Open the door. Was it last night or the night before that he stayed up and watched a movie? He cursed his routines, causing each day to blend too easily into the next. Nothing seemed wrong, nothing seemed off, other than falling asleep fully clothed. Inspecting the rest of his body, Robert found no other signs of trauma or blood. He studied his hands again, willing them to tell him their story. But they said nothing.

---

"Do you like to order for yourself?"

Piper paused before lowering the menu. She kept hidden there behind its walls, her eyes still lingering on the description for the House Style Apple Chicken Burger. For a moment, she thought she must have misheard Alex. Maybe she had misinterpreted his words over the loud hubbub of the busy brewery on a Saturday night. Because there was no way he just asked her that question on their very first date.

"I said, do you like to order for yourself, or not?" Alex repeated louder, leaning forward.

Piper laid down the menu, her lips pressed together into thin lines. She already had a splitting headache from the top knot pinned to her scalp. Piper had to hand it to herself, she actually looked pretty attractive in her slip cotton dress and leather jacket. Her boots were the only thing keeping her legs warm on that damp December evening. Except now she felt a flush come over her face. "Yes, I order for myself. I'm not a child."

Alex smirked. Piper had to hand it to him, he actually looked rather handsome in his dark jeans with a button up shirt tucked beneath his charcoal gray sweater. His thick brown hair was more elevated than usual with a generous shellac of gel, shimmering like a dark stream of crystals beneath the strands of the twinkling Christmas lights overhead.

"Everyone's different. That's why I asked."

"Every woman is different, I assume you mean? Because I guarantee you wouldn't ask a man that question," Piper snapped. She thought she felt her top knot gain a few inches from her bristling.

"Well, now I've done it," Alex laughed. "Offended you within five minutes, that must be a new record for me. Can I at least order the appetizer? Only because I'm starving, nothing to do with you being part of the fairer sex, I swear." He held up his right hand as though under oath.

Piper smiled and raised her glass in acknowledgment. She reminded herself that she wasn't disappointed in his appearance that evening, eyeing him from behind the foam of her dark porter.

After ordering dinner and another round of porter, Piper felt her body language change. She had unclasped her hands and was sitting further back in her chair, laughing so hard at times that her stomach began to hurt. She was surprised at how well this was going. She had only agreed to this date for two reasons; she thought Alex was attractive and she wanted to find out more about Robert's case. So far only one reason had been fulfilled.

"So, how's work?" Piper asked, nodding to the waitress who removed her finished plate.

"Things were going so well, are we already out of subjects?"

"I'm just curious, it's a natural thing to ask."

Alex wiped his mouth with a napkin and smiled. "Well, there will always be bad guys out there, right? Never a dull moment."

Piper pressed on. "Any big cases you're working on?"

Alex rested his hands atop the table. He began to crack his knuckles, one at a time. "I'm still new in homicide but I have a fair load. Some interesting cases." He studied Piper's face without blinking.

Piper took a sip of her water. "Anything special?"

Alex raised an eyebrow.

"I mean, anyone I might recognize?"

"Okay," Alex sighed, sitting back in his chair. "This is about Soy Latte Robert, right?"

"What?" Piper feigned surprise, badly.

"Robert Castle," Alex repeated firmly. He wondered how many more times in his life he would have to say that name.

Piper cleared her throat. She only half looked up at Alex's face, who was visibly constructing an extra layer of defense before her very eyes. "I'll admit it," she began slowly. "That I recognized you as the investigator on his case. I'm just curious about him, I see the man practically every day. He's like a weird sort of enigma."

Alex stared at her for a few more beats. Piper could guess the thoughts that were going through his head, a mixture of suspicion and training with a dash of hope she was truly just curious. They sat in a silent bubble, surrounded by the dull blur of a dozen different conversations.

"A weird sort of enigma," Alex repeated, his jaw set. "The man is a killer. He murdered his own wife."

"That was never…"

"You didn't see the body," Alex interrupted. "You don't know the details. And I don't need another person reminding me that he got off."

Silence stretched across the table. Piper looked away and chewed on her lip, bitterly wishing she hadn't mentioned Robert. But she couldn't help herself.

Finally, Alex spoke up. "Do you have a thing for him?" he asked flatly.

"Excuse me?" Piper scoffed, fire burning in her eyes.

"I'm just curious, it's a natural thing to ask, isn't it?"

Piper took a long drink of water. The waitress came and dropped off the check. Once she was gone, Piper decided to respond. "You don't know anything about me other than I can order my own dinner. But I know all I need to know about you. You are a total ass."

"I'm sorry," Alex sighed, leaning forward to reach for her hand.

Piper withdrew both hands quickly and placed them under the table.

A crack appeared in Alex's controlled demeanor. He shook his head. "You're right, that was wrong," he admitted, looking up at her warmly. "But I can't help myself when it comes to you."

"I'm ready to leave. Can we leave?" Piper stood up and straightened her jacket, fumbling for her purse that had become tangled around her chair.

Outside, the air was so crisp and cold it almost hurt to inhale. The cloudy evening sky blocked out any sign of stars as the street lamps reflected across the damp streets. Piper wrapped her leather jacket around herself tightly as though it was a suit of armor.

"I'm glad to give you a ride. Seriously," Alex insisted, pushing his hands deep into his pockets as he felt for the cigarette carton. "I don't feel real great about how we ended that."

Piper shook her head, avoiding eye contact. She bounced up and down to stay warm. "No, it's fine." She finally looked up at him.

"It was my first case," Alex admitted. "It was personal."

"Thank you for dinner," Piper said, turning to leave.

Alex reached out and hugged her, rubbing her back. She thought he kissed her on the head, but she wasn't sure. "Thank you for a wonderful evening," he sighed as he released her. His face displayed his obvious disappointment with how the night had ended and how, yet again, another part of his life was affected by Robert Castle.

Piper turned and walked down the whispering streets briskly towards her apartment. She fought back at the tears quickly emerging in her eyes, stinging with embarrassment over a good date gone bad and how, yet again, she knew nothing more about the sad man with the soy lattes.

# 200 DAYS DEAD

The first time Robert saw a raccoon, it was in his grandfather's backyard. The old man lived in the woods, a strange place to a young city boy who only knew the manicured limbs of playground trees. The trees in this place were wild and free, hiding secrets in their thick underbrush. They scared him and intrigued him at the same time. It was early morning and young Robert was eating cereal at the kitchen table. The cereal crunched, crunched, crunched between his teeth. Then he saw the creature, lumbering across the dewy grass. He blinked, rubbing his eyes. Large but strangely coordinated, the raccoon investigated a nearby trashcan then was gone as quickly as he had appeared, disappearing into the thick darkness with all its mysteries.

But Robert had never seen a raccoon this close. Limp and lifeless, it was pressed against the curb in its last futile attempt at escape from the wild road. This raccoon was much leaner than the animal of his childhood memories and Robert assumed that is what drew it into the depths of the city. Although its fur was clumped with blood, he could still see the streaks of white and gray, magnificently woven into the thick layers of black. Robert wanted to touch the dead animal with his bare hands, to satisfy that childhood curiosity once and for all. But he didn't. Drawing looks from passerby's, Robert bent down and nudged the creature into his backpack with the tip of his shoe. Once there was a break in traffic, he sprinted across the street and entered Avenue Coffee with a burst of cold air.

The coffee shop was very crowded. Usually he could avoid the majority of the prework rush, but Robert was a bit off schedule due to the distraction on his morning walk. He couldn't help it, now his eyes were drawn to that spot on the road ever since he found the dead kitten. It was like an animal death trap, as though the creatures were sickly lured there only to be struck down by one of the passing cars. This time, Robert did not want to wait until the cover of night to retrieve the corpse, allowing it to become worn down again and again by the onslaught of never-ending vehicles. He gripped the straps of his backpack tightly, shielding the little body within it.

Piper caught his eye through the sea of people, eyebrow raised. She nodded to him and started his drink. Robert's lateness had thrown off her entire schedule, causing her to miss her break since she always took it after he left with his soy latte. And now he was here late. Piper studied Robert as she prepared his drink, particularly the backpack that he cradled over his shoulder.

"What happened to you?" she asked, delivering his soy latte even though the line of patrons was quickly accumulating.

"I'm sorry, I don't think I have time to wait in line to pay. And I don't have cash. I have to use card. But I'm going to be late to work if I have to wait in line," Robert explained breathlessly, grasping the hot cup. This was his one normal thing in this already strange morning and he craved it. He shifted the backpack on his shoulder and looked around.

Piper waved her hand, dismissing the charge for the coffee she never rang up. "Don't worry about it. It's fine." She looked him up and down. "And you're okay? It's very unlike you to be late. Or, I guess it's very unlike you."

Robert paused and stared at Piper. He wondered, just for a second, if it would be acceptable to tell her that he had a dead raccoon in his backpack. "It's just been a strange morning," he finally replied, holding up the soy latte in acknowledgment. He started to walk away and stopped. "And thanks."

Robert kept his backpack in his locker at work. He thought about it all day, wondering if he should go and check on it during his short lunch break. Maybe the body would start to reek of death. Maybe someone would complain about the smell and management would enact a locker search and they would find his mysterious backpack with a dead raccoon inside. All day while he toiled, Robert imagined up excuses he could use if it came to it. He even whispered them to himself, testing how the words sounded together, but nothing ever truly made sense. When the bell rang at 5:00, Robert kept his head down and walked across the murky port towards home.

Standing on the front steps of his house, Robert hesitated before going inside. He knew Jasper was probably sleeping, one ear perked up and listening for his master's return. Due to his previous experience with Jasper and a dead animal, Robert wanted to avoid another night of endless whining and scratching at the door. Remembering the flashlight on his keychain, Robert stumbled around the side of the house to the small plot of earth where he had buried the kitten. He carefully opened his backpack, the stench from the corpse releasing into the air. Unintentionally, his hand brushed against the coarse fur of the raccoon and for a moment, it felt warm.

Robert had left the small garden shovel propped up against the house from his last burial. He placed the backpack carefully on the ground, reaching in the darkness for the first grave to find placement for the next. The soil felt moist. Fresh. Loose. His heart leapt as he directed his flashlight to the kitten's grave. Jasper must have gotten to it and Robert feared he had left the kitten's corpse to a fate worse than the roadway. But as he inspected the soil, Robert did not see any claw marks or signs of disarray.

He began to dig. Furiously, outraged that someone may be playing games with this sacred little sanctuary he had conjured up on his property. When the brown paper bag began to poke out from the loose soil, Robert tugged it free and found it empty. He held it, light as air, until allowing the bag to flutter to the ground. Had the kitten decomposed that quickly? There was no way. He began to sift through the soil with his bare hands, the earth cool and velvety. It ran between his fingers but he never struck the sharp bones or coarse fur he was expecting. The kitten's corpse was gone.

Robert sat back on his heels, pushing his hair out of his face. It was cold but he was sweating, heavily. *Who could have done this? Why?* He felt sick. He was fairly sure no one had seen him bury the kitten those weeks ago under the evening sky. His neighbors didn't even have a view of this side of the house. It must have been another animal. He thought about Jasper and his uncouth ways. *Not him.* None of his neighbors had outdoor pets that he knew of. No wandering animals that he could recall. The only creature who came to mind was the orange and white kitten who appeared that sunny afternoon in his backyard, chasing an elusive fly. Robert paused and looked in the empty brown paper sack again. He lowered it slowly. *Except for that orange and white kitten.*

Scooping up the backpack, Robert rushed inside the house. As expected, Jasper heard his master, smelled the dead raccoon, and came howling down the hallway. Robert placed his backpack atop the refrigerator and reached with shaky hands for the whiskey bottle he kept there as well, as though he had to keep the alcohol out of someone's reach. Jasper barked and lunged towards the backpack, his nails scratching down the textured plastic of the refrigerator doors. The burn of the whiskey helped to calm Robert's racing heart. He took a few more swigs then promptly replaced the bottle atop the refrigerator.

He didn't believe in ghosts. If he had, Robert would have believed that Claire haunted the hallways of their home. He always heard different creaks and cracks or imagined objects in the house had moved or been replaced. He sat on the couch in the dark living room, reevaluating everything. Suddenly, Robert felt overwhelmingly small. He was going to go outright and say it to himself. *Was that kitten the same kitten? It couldn't be. Could it?*

Jasper's jumping antics knocked a bowl off the countertop, sending large pieces of porcelain across the kitchen floor. The loud crash snapped Robert out of his distracted buzz as he ushered Jasper outside and began sweeping up the chunky shards. He whispered to himself as he swept, thinking through and rationalizing all the bizarre thoughts that were flittering through his mind. The kitten had been there. The kitten was gone. Someone or something had probably taken the kitten. Simple as that.

Once the remains of the bowl were cleaned up, Robert grabbed the backpack and went out through the back door, brushing past Jasper who jumped and snapped at the smell of death. Turning the corner, Robert bent down at his makeshift burial site and began to dig a new grave with his bare hands. He stuffed the backpack and raccoon inside the hole and scooped the soil back on top. A small bump in the ground remained once he was finished, having done a poor job of digging a deep enough hole. Robert also stuffed the empty paper bag back in the kitten's grave and patted it down firmly. He wiped the sweat from his forehead and looked over at Jasper, who had been watching from a cautious distance.

"Leave it," Robert ordered loudly, pointing at the two graves.

Jasper barked, twirled in a circle, and ran off.

Robert stood up and brushed off his clothes. He was feeling the whiskey and the exhaustion of the day. He wouldn't keep doing this. He couldn't. Taking one last look at the ground, he walked away and went to bed. He dreamed that his floating house was in a sea of graves, rocking back and forth precariously, on the verge of toppling over at any moment.

---

The dead leaves crunched between Robert's gloved fingertips. He pulled at them hard, dropping the remains into a growing pile of crumbling winter plants that should have been cleared out long before. Why Claire had insisted on planting these flowers, he did not know. She wasn't a flower person, especially an annual flower like this. He didn't even know the plant's type or name, just that its time was done and had to go.

He yanked on it hard and the brittle base of the plant snapped, leaving the roots hidden below the soil. Robert muttered as he rummaged through his box of yard tools.

The sky on that afternoon was a very Seattle cocktail of gray. It was typical winter weather, dark with a hint of drizzle. The air was damp and musky, with a hint of the muted aroma of discarded Christmas trees on the streets waiting for pickup. Jasper inspected the pile of dead flowers and vines that had collected on the backyard patio. Robert began tossing miscellaneous garden tools out of his yard box.

"What'd you do with the shovel?" Robert asked Jasper. One day, Robert counted how many times he talked to Jasper. It was more than it should have been.

Jasper did not recognize any keywords that were of importance to him and continued rummaging through the pile of soon-to-be compost.

The drizzle was slowly turning into rain. Random droplets became heavier and heavier, denser and denser. The rain hastened Robert to complete his task as he continued his hunt for the shovel, stopping at the far edge of his house. Right around the corner was the little graveyard, still containing one occupant and an empty paper bag. He hadn't been back since he buried the raccoon and he didn't know why. He chalked it up to having no business over there but truly he knew that wasn't the reason. He didn't like that night. He didn't like the strange thoughts that had wandered through his mind. And now as his thoughts meandered back, he remembered the little garden shovel, probably still propped up against the house. The rain fell heavier, harder. He needed the shovel to finish this task. He was going to get it. Jasper looked up but didn't follow him.

The side of the house was just as Robert had left it. Soil was scattered across the cement pathway, now melting into streams of mud. He stopped in front of the two graves and picked up the small garden shovel. He couldn't help but let his eyes fall to the soil and the sweat began to gather along with the rain on his neck. The kitten's grave looked fine, the firm soil still packed down as he had left it. But the once raised earth of the messy grave dug for the raccoon now was flat. The ground appeared level instead of the bump due to the full backpack. A corner of fabric poked out through the loose soil. Robert's hands began to shake as he reached down to touch it. A backpack strap. He pulled on the strap, releasing it from beneath the earth. Robert held the backpack in front of his face as soil scattered to the ground. *Empty.*

In that waning, wet light of day, Robert inspected the bag carefully. The faint smell of dead carcass still lingered. He reached his hand inside and pulled out clumps of white, black, and gray hair. His hand was caked with dried blood. That raccoon had been real, the tangible evidence was now literally on his fingertips. Leaving the pile of dead plants on his patio, Robert stomped back into his house, backpack in hand. Jasper followed him and watched as he left it on the kitchen countertop.

Robert picked up his car keys. He pointed at the backpack. "Leave it. I mean it," he ordered Jasper.

Jasper laid down with a clank of his collar on the hardwood floors. It was an hour later when Robert returned. Jasper had been dutifully waiting in the kitchen, guarding the suspicious but empty backpack. In the last remains of day, Robert installed security cameras on the side of his house, pointed directly at the little gravesite. He adjusted the devices obsessively until the chill of the dark rain drove him inside. Robert changed out of his wet clothes and slept hard that night, a heavy, dreamless sleep that woke him at a very early hour of the morning.

Stumbling out of bed, Robert went straight to review the security camera recordings from the night before. He scanned through the grainy yellow night vision footage, unsure what he was looking for or not looking for. Yesterday, he had concluded someone must be vandalizing his property and he knew from his experience with law enforcement that he needed real physical proof.

Robert stopped the footage at around 3:00 am. He rubbed the sleep out of his eyes and scanned it back and forth several times. There was a small amount of movement in the corner of the camera's reach, so slight that Robert was amazed he even caught it. The small creature was definitely not human, scurrying as it scratched along the edge of the fence line. The footage continued and Robert felt the hairs on the back of his neck stand up, one at a time. A pudgy little animal wobbled over to the two graves. It hesitated and appeared to look at the camera, then wobbled away again. Although the form was a blur, Robert still knew what he was looking at, as though he was that boy in his grandfather's house again, meeting the gaze of the creature in the dewy backyard grass.

# 214 DAYS DEAD

"Bobby's here! Hey, Shannon! Bobby's here!"

Robert could hear Grant's booming voice through the closed front door, his hand mid-air as he prepared to knock. The crisp white paint on the door was so clean and new it almost blinded him. Everything about this housing development was clean and new.

"Welcome to Snoqualmie!" Grant shouted as he opened the door, enveloping Robert in a firm hug. He smelled like he had just got out of the shower, likely having slept in after a late night at the restaurant. His clothes were perfectly pressed and his thick brown hair glistened with more evidence of a recent shower. Robert looked down at his own disheveled jeans, oversized sweater, and stained jacket. Grant let go quickly and held his friend at arm's length. "My God, man. Lost some weight?"

"Don't. Of course, he has," a woman's voice chided from the shadows. Grant's wife, Shannon, appeared in the doorway. She was dressed in a long kimono-like dress with a heavy sweater over it. Robert had never seen her with gray hair but now it had erupted all around her hairline, like a crown of ashen snow. He couldn't help but look at her slightly bulging stomach, one of the reasons for his celebratory trip to his old friend's new house. They had wanted a baby for a long time. Both couples had.

"Congratulations, Shan." Robert kissed her cheek. He hadn't kissed a woman's cheek in a long time. It startled him how soft it was.

Grant grabbed Robert by the shoulders and walked him inside. "Come in, man! How was the drive? Don't you love this air out here? Man, I can finally breathe!"

Shannon followed them into the kitchen, apologizing for the boxes and picking up scattered trash along the way. Grant ushered his friend to the large glass doors that opened into the impressive backyard, pointing out the locations for his barbecue pit and sandbox for the future baby. Robert couldn't begrudge them their happiness. He remembered the excitement he and Claire had shared over their first house. Their first real house that was all their own. There was nothing like it.

"How are you?" Shannon asked Robert over lunch. She was piling a huge mountain of lettuce on Robert's plate, smothering it with toppings and dressing. The friends were gathered around the kitchen table, eating out of plastic bowls and with chopsticks left from the previous night's take out.

Robert focused on opening his can of soda before answering. It popped open loudly and a small gathering of bubbles threatened to overflow. He nodded and shrugged at the same time. "It's hard, sometimes."

"At least everything has calmed down in the papers and such," Shannon added, watching his reaction from under her heavy bangs. "I hated that. I hated it. So unfair. Why is it always the spouse that's suspected? Isn't it horrible enough that it happened? Why?"

"Scumbags," Grant mumbled through a large bite of romaine.

"Are you eating? Maybe you should eat out more, I know Claire usually...well…" Shannon's voice trailed off. Her eyes welled with tears at the mention of her dead friend's name.

"Don't get upset. It's not good. No more talk of Claire," Grant whispered to his wife. He turned to Robert. "Unless you want to talk about it more, Bobby."

Robert shook his head. He had been experiencing a version of this conversation over and over again with numerous well-meaning acquaintances. At first, the outpourings Robert had received about Claire's death were of horror and support. And as much as they would deny it, then they would doubt. Then they felt anger and pity. Finally, avoidance.

"It's fine," Robert said. He had learned this was all he should say and to leave it at that. To say he was moving on would cause a raise of an eyebrow. To say he missed her every second of the day would solicit furrowed glances.

Grant sighed loudly, pushing his plate away. "Let's turn this around. We got a surprise planned for you, bud." He thumped Robert hard on the back. "We're going to Snoqualmie Falls! And I'm driving!"

Sitting in the backseat of Grant's large black Suburban, Robert gripped his seatbelt and stared out the window. He didn't have the heart or energy to admit that he had seen Snoqualmie Falls before and that sitting in the backseat made him carsick. Grant and Shannon chatted loudly over the radio, pointing out various attractions on the windy road to the majestic waterfall. Robert looked over at the empty seat beside him, already occupied by an infant's car seat. He reached over and touched it.

"Don't look!" Grant called out to Shannon suddenly.

As Shannon groaned and covered her eyes, Robert peered ahead into the roadway. The Suburban passed by a dead deer on the side of the road, a splatter of bright red blood noticeable on the pavement. Quickly turning in his seat, Robert watched through the rear window as the corpse of the deer disappeared into the distance. The animal's head had been twisted in the accident, just enough to give Robert one long last look before the Suburban turned a corner and was gone.

"This girl," Grant called back, shaking his head. "She can't take anything right now. Gets teary about spilled milk, literally."

"Poor deer," Shannon lamented, crying anyway.

She continued to cry for the remainder of the drive to Snoqualmie Falls and half of the visit there. Huge tears, almost like the water droplets that rushed over the mountainside and crashed to the ground below. Robert began to wonder if it would have been better to let Shannon see the deer for herself, if the unknown was conjuring up a worse image than reality. She was asleep in the car by the time they passed the deer again on their journey home. Robert watched the carcass flash by, willing himself not to look back.

Sitting on the back patio, Robert and Grant ate leftover Chinese food and split the last beer from the fridge. Shannon had long since gone to bed, even though the sun was still setting in the far horizon. The two men talked about their jobs and laughed over old times from college. Robert had not laughed like that for a long time.

"I hope you had a good time, man. Just wanted to get you some good fresh air, you know?" Grant said, crunching the empty beer can in his hand. He tossed it into a nearby recycling can with ease. "And Shannon, well, this is hard on her."

Robert noticed the strain in his friend's voice. "Really?"

Grant stared straight ahead. "She gets weird pain sometimes. Makes her scared. Well, scares me too. Doctor says everything looks normal. But after how long it's been, you can't help it, you know?"

Robert could not think up a response. Even with the miscarriages of his own, even with the thoughtful regrets that had been offered to him, he still couldn't find the right words for the fear that his friend was battling. Grant covered his face and groaned into his fingers.

"Bobby. God, I'm sorry," Grant whispered. "I don't know why. But I forget sometimes. Maybe because I knew you before Claire? I dunno, it's no excuse. I have nothing to complain about, I know it." He hesitated before continuing, carefully choosing his next words. "I've been meaning to ask you. How are you doing...really?"

Robert still said nothing. Beneath the surface reasons for his visit to Grant and Shannon's laid the real motive. He envisioned a moment just like this, where he could tell another living creature besides Jasper what was going on in his life. What was *really* going on in his life. He sat forward in his chair, the stiff fabric creaking beneath his weight. Rubbing his face in his hands, Robert felt his stomach drop. "No," he finally choked. "I don't think I'm…right."

Grant leaned forward as well. "Go on, man."

Robert shook his head. He couldn't say the words. They sounded so absurd, so ridiculous, he didn't even know how to start a sentence like that. He didn't know how to say he believed he was bringing dead animals back to life. And that he had evidence of it, in a way, on that blurry security camera tape. Unless that wasn't real, either.

Clearing his throat, Grant fumbled to find Robert's words for him. "Are you…um, feeling sad? I mean, you're not going to hurt yourself, are you, man?"

Robert shook his head.

"Okay," Grant sighed. "Is it trouble sleeping? Nightmares?"

"In a way, yes. But not."

"C'mon, just spit it out, man."

Robert started and stopped a few times before finally answering. He felt like every living thing surrounding that back yard held its breath, from the faraway crickets to the moths fluttering against the porch light. Pausing and watching and waiting to see if he would really say it. Robert turned and looked Grant straight in the face. "I find dead animals. And they come back to life."

Grant obviously had not prepared himself for that answer. He struggled to control his expression completely, to reveal nothing that could possibly discourage his fragile friend. Robert exhaled loudly, the pressure in his stomach finally relaxing. He had released the words, the thoughts, into the ether. But he did not know where they would take him now.

"Ghosts?" Grant tried to clarify, blinking once. "You're seeing animal ghosts?"

"They're real," Robert replied firmly. "Alive. Alive again."

Grant sat back in his chair. He looked around the dark patio as though trying to find the next thing to say. He chose rationalization. "So, you find dead animals. And you keep them?"

"Bury them."

"Okay. Okay, that's normal," Grant reasoned. "And then?"

"They somehow escape the grave. Dig out, crawl out, evaporate out…I don't know. Then they come back. Alive." Robert himself felt alive being able to discuss this so freely.

Grant rubbed his eyes hard. "This is where you're losing me, bud."

"Trust me," Robert said flatly. "You and me both."

The patio door burst open and both men jumped out of their seats. Shannon appeared in the doorway, her hair sticking out in a dozen different directions. Her face was limp with fatigue.

"Babe, you good?" Grant asked. "What's going on?"

"Shut up and come to bed," she mumbled firmly. "Your voices are annoying me. Night, Robert." She turned and lumbered back upstairs.

Grant and Robert said quiet goodbyes on their way to the front door.

"Man, I gotta think about what you told me," Grant whispered, looking over his shoulder at the stairway. "Maybe you need to come out here more, you know? Remember what I was saying about that fresh air? Clean your head out more often?"

Robert shrugged. Obviously releasing the words had done no good.

Grant studied his old friend's face, squinting in the insufficient light. "Are you serious about this?"

"I don't know," Robert said with a sigh. "I'll talk to you later."

Grant waved a silent goodbye and carefully shut and locked the door behind him. Robert watched from the damp night grass as the lights in the house trickled off one by one as Grant made his way upstairs to bed. Robert's car was glistening beneath the street lamp that hummed overhead. He unlocked the door and stooped inside. While the front windshield defrosted, Robert stared at the blank section of fresh concrete illuminated by his headlights. His mind began to wander back to the dead deer, splattered across a section of concrete much like the one before him, the memory scratching at the corners of his mind. Wiping away the remaining condensation with his coat sleeve, Robert drove down the road towards Snoqualmie Falls.

The murky forest was unfamiliar to him. He had spent too long in the city and now the thick darkness made the hairs on his arms stand at alert. Finally, his headlights caught the still form of the lifeless deer. Robert pulled over and left his car idling, sitting in the darkness. He was waiting for that moment when he questioned what he was doing. But it never came.

The constant rain had washed away any trace of blood from the roadway. Robert knelt down and studied the face of the deer, seeing now it was a stag. The animal looked strangely peaceful to him, its blank eyes forever staring towards a lush meadow in its dreams. Carefully, he touched the stag's coarse fur. It felt cold. His fingers trailed up to the animal's antlers, old and mysterious. He had probably been the first human to touch them. And he would be the last.

As he had not planned for having to bury a large corpse, Robert's only digging tool was the ice scraper from his trunk. Choosing a location at the edge of the forest, he dug a hole that he estimated would be just deep enough to hold the animal. The task seemed to take him forever, as Robert would stop and fall motionless each time a car sped by. Finally, Robert dragged the deer's surprisingly heavy body to the edge of the grave and hesitated. He reached into his coat pocket and pulled out the decorative Snoqualmie Falls pin that Grant had insisted on buying him at the gift shop. Robert pricked the pin into the stag's left ear and rolled the body into the grave.

Driving home, the passing headlights leered at Robert's racing thoughts. His actions were making his heart pound a little harder, making him take a solid look at who he was becoming. He was a man that comforted others about the murder of his own wife and spent his spare time burying roadkill. And now it was escalating. Now he had gone out of his way to bury that deer and with a marker, no less. Robert gripped the steering wheel harder and harder until his hands went numb. He had to hold onto something.

---

His moments with coffee in the morning were glorious. They were somehow the one thing that made him still feel human. A magic liquid that could summon light out of the coldest soul. Robert took a heavy breath and blew sleepy air over his steaming mug of black coffee. The warmth from the cup tried to compete with the damp chill of the early morning kitchen and it was winning, sip by sip. Robert had awoken at his normal time, following his usual routine and beginning to pack his lunch for the day. When he heard the last burst of steam and the final click of his coffee pot, Robert stopped everything to lean against the kitchen sink and look out the window with that warm cup of liquid courage. Adjusting to the day, sip by sip.

He heard Jasper start to rustle, the clicking of his nails across the wood floors and the loud slobbery licks from his water bowl. Jasper had a morning routine, too. Robert was starting to see signs of Jasper's age creeping up on him. How he had to stretch after getting out of bed or take that extra moment of hesitation before jumping up into it at night. Robert wondered if Jasper was becoming aware of it, if he woke up one day and looked at his reflection in the water bowl and saw the small gray hairs. Smiling, Robert walked over to the kitchen table and began to look for Jasper's leash through the various papers and old mail that had collected there.

Movement outside the glass sliding door caught his eye. Robert's response time was considerably delayed from the lack of caffeine in his system but he could make out the slow, deliberate steps. The deer sniffed around the empty planter boxes and licked at the gathered dew. Slowly, Robert walked towards the glass door until his face was almost pressed against it. In the quiet of the early morning, he could even hear the stag's footsteps on the misty cement patio. The animal became aware of Robert and straightened, falling completely motionless other than his heavy breathing and the twitching of his nose. Robert stared at the animal without breathing, his eyes focused on that wet nose, trembling with life. Jasper came trotting down the hallway and joined Robert at his side, apparently accustomed to these strange animals that appeared in his backyard. The stag looked down at the little dog and Robert saw the glint of a small Snoqualmie Falls Pin.

# 222 DAYS DEAD

"This is just what I needed," Zelda sighed. She took another bite of her pepperoni pizza and spoke through her chews. "Nothing like grease to calm my stomach."

"Yeah, I know!" Piper shouted louder than she needed to. Her ears were filled with a dull ring and she knew the concert had probably knocked a few years off her hearing. Behind her, she could feel the reverberations as the raging music of the band pressed against her back. They stood outside Pachelbel's Lizard, huddled beneath an overhang as the rain poured in torrents all around them like a hundred waterfalls. Pedestrians scuttled through the gathered puddles as the passing cars pressed against the storm with frantic wipers. Piper looked down at her suede boots, already soaking wet, and knew it was just going to get worse. Stray water droplets gathered on her thin leather jacket, searching for a way to get past the barrier and settle against her skin.

Seattle's music scene left nothing to be desired, especially for Piper. She had grown up in a place with no name in the rolling hills of California, a mere stop off the freeway that hadn't earned the honor of a title. There, she had gobbled up all the music she could get her hands on, listening intensely from her window as the music transported her over the dry, smooth hills. When she moved to Seattle, she ventured to different clubs and venues she had read about in magazines. There, she had devoured the uniqueness and culture she had dreamed was out there, swept away from behind her closed eyes as the music transported her across the seas of people.

Piper's phone beeped and buzzed from within her limp purse. She had brought only the staples for that night, having learned the hard way that it was too easy to lose valuables in the wild crowd. Piper glanced at her phone screen and dropped it back in her purse with panache.

"Again?" Zelda asked with raised eyebrow, moving onto the crust of her pizza. Her eyeliner was smeared down her face from a mixture of sweat, rain, and general humidity. She was dressed in black, her hair still managing to stay slick. It was outings like this that made Piper remember why she was friends with Zelda, not the sour girl that always arrived late to her shift at Avenue Coffee.

"Yes," Piper replied, louder than intended again. "Third time tonight. I told him I was busy, this is ridiculous."

"Oh well," Zelda chomped, wiping her greasy hands on the arms of her jacket. "Anyway, you're into murderers, not cops."

"Really?" Piper snapped, the droplets gathered on her leather jacket tumbling to the ground as she spun to face a snickering Zelda. "Enough. Seriously. I'm not-"

Zelda's face fell flat as she raised her hand to interrupt Piper. She pointed behind Piper's shoulder. "Speak of the devil. Look who's out for a night on the town."

Piper swung around and caught a fleeting glance of Robert as he exited Pachelbel's Lizard. The collar on his heavy jacket was pulled up high, concealing the lower part of his face. He pushed his way through the crowd gathered by the door, sliding between them smoothly. He looked out of place in his stone washed jeans and tennis shoes, yet no one seemed to notice. With his head tucked down, Robert acknowledged no one and made no eye contact. He took a sharp turn and strode down the sidewalk into the darkness. Without a word, Piper grabbed Zelda's arm and dragged her into the rainstorm after Robert.

They followed Robert for a long time. Piper took no note of street names or landmarks although she heard the occasional muttered remark from Zelda about them. She couldn't take her eyes off Robert's stooped form, as though if she blinked he would evaporate and wash away with the rain. His gait was completely different than the man she had watched enter Avenue Coffee a hundred times, different in a way that made a gnawing pit grow in Piper's stomach. That feeling she had been raised to trust, her gut, that sense that told her things that her brain and heart didn't understand. To just trust something was wrong and leave it at that. And that night, something was wrong about Robert.

"My feet are numb. Burning numb. Amputation numb," Zelda whispered sharply. Both girls were struggling to keep up with Robert, who paused for no street light or crosswalk. He just continued walking, purposefully, into the dark night.

"I know, I know," Piper replied, now attempting to keep her voice quiet. "Just a little further." Her own feet had started going numb ages ago and she regretted her stupid suede shoes with the click clacking heels. She thought for sure that Robert would turn to finally investigate the source of the obnoxious sound, but he never did.

They began to near the waterfront. Piper was vaguely familiar with this area of Seattle, but the unmistakable dampness of the nearby body of water confirmed it for her. She and Zelda both slowed their pace as Robert's stride began to change. She didn't know how to explain it, but something in Robert's shoulders made her think he finally felt safe to relax. The two girls kept a good distance from him as they sauntered past quiet, sleeping homes that floated on the edge of the waterfront. The midnight silence on that street was beautiful, marred only by the steady swing of the docks and the click clacking of Piper's heels. Then another sound joined the ranks as Robert fumbled in his pockets, pulling out a jingling set of keys. Piper gripped Zelda's freezing hand and squeezed it so hard her friend had to pull it away. They stopped in a patch of shadows and watched as Robert walked up the drive to one of the dark houses, unlocking the front door and shutting it very quietly behind him.

"So this is where he lives," Piper whispered, sounding more in awe than she intended. Her tongue was numb from using it to stop her chattering teeth.

"What a revelation," Zelda said, sounding just as bitter as she intended. "Can we call a ride now?"

"I'll give you a ride."

Piper and Zelda both screamed hoarsely and spun around. Alex was standing several feet behind them, the driver's side door to his parked car wide open. He stared at Piper flatly. "That is, if you're not still busy."

Piper felt her face burn and blamed it on a fever setting in. "What are you doing here?" she asked, straightening her soaking wet clothes.

"Who cares? I'm getting in," Zelda chattered, rushing past Alex and climbing into the backseat of his sedan.

Alex wiped the rain from his forehead. "I come here occasionally, to keep an eye on things."

"To keep an eye on Robert," Piper clarified, straining to keep her voice steady.

"Yes. Absolutely. I don't hide that at all," Alex replied. "And what's your reason for being here?"

"We got lost," Zelda shouted from the car. "And you get to be our knight in shining armor and take us home. So take us home, already."

Alex looked from Piper then over to Robert's dark house. He knelt down and started the ignition on the car, turning the heater on full blast. Walking over to the passenger side of the car, he opened the door for Piper and waited.

Piper avoided eye contact as she walked past Alex and collapsed into the warm car. She never thought she would be so happy for heated seats. Alex said nothing as he drove off down the quiet street, lights turned down low as though not to attract attention. As though he had done this many times before. Piper peered through the foggy windshield for one last look at Robert's house. She imagined him inside, soaking wet from his trek through the rain, maybe watching them, too.

---

Robert looked up from the Sunday paper, spread out all around him like a quilt of ink. Jasper laid by his owner closer than usual, his ears sporadically twitching. This storm would not let up, it had raged all week, all night, and now into Robert's coveted weekend. He glanced up at his jacket hanging on the coat hook, still dripping water into a puddle on the floor. He was beginning to wonder if he should pop it into the dryer, he didn't remember it being that soaked when he got home from work. An especially loud burst of wind rattled outside and the lights began to flicker.

"Great," he sighed. As though on cue, the lights flickered again with one last blast then died away, leaving them in deafening silence only broken by the sneering wind outside.

Crunching across the newspapers on the floor, Robert began to open the window blinds and let in the remaining light of day. Jasper followed him like a shadow. They marched around the house in this fashion, window to window. Power outages were not a rare occurrence for Robert. He decided that his house must exist in some sort of Bermuda Triangle of the electricity grid. The whole city of Seattle could have power except for his little corner of the concrete jungle.

Fumbling his way into the garage, Robert found the flashlight and began to fiddle with the breaker switches. Nothing happened. Jasper waited for him inside, unsure of that garage even when the fluorescents were on. When Robert returned, Jasper was huddled in the corner of the kitchen, his rear in the air and tail wagging wildly. Robert knew this stance too well.

"What've you got?" he called, taking his flashlight and aiming it at the corner of the floor. Jasper scooted away and revealed a small cricket, dramatically turned on its side with one spindly leg in the air as though poised for flight. Robert flicked it carefully with his finger and confirmed the insect was dead.

Jasper sat several feet back, remembering the harsh words his previous interactions with tiny insects had elicited from his owner. Robert crouched down and studied the cricket gently. He followed each line from top to bottom, noting the variations in color and the delicate antennae. The hot beam from the flashlight made certain fragments of the insect almost translucent. Robert squinted his eyes and looked closer. A tiny mass was visible in the insect's chest cavity. A mass of cells intertwined together, still quivering from the recent bursts of life. *Was it a heart?*

Sitting back, Robert rubbed his face hard. Insects don't have hearts. At least, not the kind pumping in a chest cavity. He laid on his stomach and pointed the flashlight beam at the dead cricket once more. Again, he could identify a tiny shape in the chest cavity area of the insect, a dense mass with veiny strings that spread through the cricket like a circulatory system.

Robert and Jasper laid on the kitchen floor for a long time, watching the cricket. Eventually, the sun began to set and the heavy flashlight beam became the only source of light. Robert could not take his eyes off the cricket. He began to do things like willing the cricket back to life, whatever that meant. Or imagining the cricket's heart beating again, blood flowing through the insect in a cartoonish manner. Then he held his finger on the cricket and counted to ten, wondering if he had a magic touch that could spurn a creature back to life. Nothing happened.

Robert thought about the kitten. And the raccoon. And finally the stag, buried at the side of the road only to break free and find that lush meadow, after all. *Buried.* They had all been buried. Jumping up, Robert grabbed a small pot from the windowsill that was home to a very small patch of cilantro. Nudging over a bit of dirt, Robert created a tiny grave for the limp insect. He picked up the cricket with a spatula, afraid to tear the thin flesh, and dropped it in the hole. Robert patted the soil back over the cricket's grave, at rest beside the quiet forest of herbs.

Robert prepared for bed, gripping the flashlight beneath his chin and pointing the beam towards the waterfall of cold sink water. It was then that he noticed the outline of ink on the inside of his right wrist. Faint, almost erased by the hand washing of the day, the imprint revealed itself in the concentrated beam of the flashlight. Robert inspected his wrist closer, trying to make sense of the fluid form depicted in pale green ink. Finally he joined Jasper in bed, who was already nestled beneath the layers of blankets in search of warmth. Robert rubbed his wrist and listened to the ticking of the clock on the wall, minute by minute, second by second, until finally he drifted off to sleep. He woke heavily hours later. The power was still off and Jasper's snoring was significantly muffled due to his position beneath the covers.

Then, he heard it. A faint chirp, far away yet still audible in the silent house. Robert sat up straight and listened closer. He heard it again. Racing down the hallway, Robert stumbled through the darkness towards the kitchen. There was enough ambient light coming in through the windows to make out basic shapes and forms. Reaching the pot on the windowsill, Robert inspected it. The small grave was open, tiny scratch marks drawn through the loose soil. Robert jumped as the cricket chirped loudly from the window glass, squeezing outside through a small gap in the frame. It fluttered and flew away, summoned by a chorus of other chirps, calling to it from somewhere in the night.

---

Piper knew she was dreaming but she went along with it. She willed herself to keep going, to keep exploring this strange house she found herself in. In her dream, Piper had awoken in a warm, sunny room. A room that was a strange concoction of the guest room at her grandmother's house and Piper's old dorm room. Long morning shadows stretched across the carpet, leading her sleepy eyes towards a steep staircase. As she climbed out of the tall, fluffy bed and walked towards the stairs, Piper heard her alarm buzzing in the far, faint distance. She slid her hand against the wallpaper as she descended the staircase. She felt the ridges and valleys and tiny tears beneath her fingertips as she took each step. She must have instinctively snoozed the alarm as Piper no longer heard the buzzing as she entered a kitchen. It took her eyes a few moments to absorb the abnormally bright room. Piper saw a figure at the stove, standing in front of a sizzling pan. As her eyes adjusted, she recognized the tall, lanky form.

"Robert?" she whispered.

He did not turn around. She stepped closer but he was completely oblivious to her, humming to himself and stirring the food in the pan. Piper turned around and looked at the bright light coming through the oversized sliding glass doors. She walked closer, shielding her eyes. There was another form outside, familiar to Piper again by his tall, lanky outline. Another Robert? A dozen limbs stretched from his torso, writhing into the air. Figures that Piper could not identify walked around him. This version of Robert noticed Piper and turned to look at her with dark eyes. She went paralyzed as he raised his hand and reached towards her. A chill ran from the top to the bottom of her spine as she felt herself be drawn to him. She floated helplessly through the air, the sliding glass door shattering before her skin made contact. Piper could feel the heat emanating from him, building with ferocity. He pulled Piper so close that she thought her skin would melt from her bones and then everything blurred to a burning white.

Piper sat up with a start as the alarm on her cell phone cut through the air. She reached over and picked up the vibrating phone with her trembling hand. She was drenched in a cold sweat. She played back through every moment of the dream, straining to put together the pieces before they slipped through her fingers. Her phone continued to ring alerts even though Piper had turned off her alarm. They were messages from Zelda. Many, many messages from Zelda.

*omg*
*Did you see??????? Last night?*
*Are you AWAKE? There was a MURDER at the club!!*
*Was it your soy latte guy?*

Piper threw down the phone and searched the news for information on the murder. Zelda was right, there had been a murder, in the minutes before or after the two girls had trailed Robert all the way home. Piper didn't need to know who died. Her hands felt numb. She tried to think back to those moments at Pachelbel's Lizard, but she could remember nothing but loud, clattering music. A knot began to knit in Piper's stomach, a small pebble that started to take shape and slowly spread.

Piper rushed through her morning routine. After a quick shower and changing into her outfit for the day, she peered at the storm outside and reached for her heavy rain jacket. She had to go to work, even if her feet were still torn to shreds, she had a splitting headache, and her strange night of sleep was anything but restful. On her walk to work, the sidewalks had become congested with rivers of rain runoff, twisting and curving their way across the concrete in search of the sea. Piper was scheduled for the second wave of the morning crew as she had enough seniority to avoid the dreaded 4:00 am opening shift. By the time Robert would arrive for his soy latte, Piper will have been there long enough to compose herself. But this morning, she wanted nothing more but to be back in bed. To put her feet up and think. And dream.

Piper stopped at the crosswalk and felt her shoulders get heavier as the rain beat down harder and harder. She was so tired of this rain. Staring at the ground from beneath her hood, Piper saw the feet of her fellow pedestrians join her side, waiting for the crosswalk light to turn. It would be the last thing she remembered seeing for a very long time.

# 224 DAYS DEAD

Robert had walked this route to work for a long time. Early on, he began to recognize the passing faces of his fellow walking commuters, all seeming to be on the same schedule. Although they never introduced themselves or truly made eye contact, still these pedestrians and Robert knew each other. When one of them was missing, he wondered if they were sick or simply gone. Because sometimes people did do that. Sometimes they were simply just gone.

This morning was different. Robert could feel it already. The torrential rain was causing the world to look submerged. He and his fellow pedestrians were just souls walking underwater, sluggish and blurred, unrecognizable although familiar. Even the storefronts he passed every morning looked different to Robert. He wasn't that surprised when he came upon an unusual crowd a few blocks from Avenue Coffee, a gathering of heavy coats on their cell phones, even in the midst of the rain. Stepping around the crowd, Robert glanced in passing at the subject of their interest. He stopped when he saw Piper laying on the ground.

Shoving his way in, Robert knelt next to Piper on the wet street. She was a crumpled mess beneath her heavy coat, curled in a twisted version of the fetal position. Blood was mixing in with her eyeliner, a strange blend of black and red tears streaming down her face. Robert felt her face. It was ice cold.

"What happened?" Robert shouted at the crowd, looking around until focusing in on the nearest person, a man in a long black suit and holding a long umbrella.

The man looked around to see if Robert was addressing him, then answered loudly through the beating rain. "I don't know! I was walking by and found her like this!"

"It was a car! A car hit her, then drove off!" another voice chimed in.

"I'm on hold with the police!"

"Is she still alive? Poor girl!"

Robert touched Piper's cold face again. He searched for a pulse and found nothing. He studied her eyes, wide and blank. He wondered if she was afraid. He felt his pulse start to pick up. His stomach lurched. He was having a physical reaction to the thought that was about to pop into his head. To what he was about to attempt to do.

"I've got her. I'll take care of it!" Robert shouted, struggling to pick up Piper's limp body.

A flush of whispers circled through the crowd.

"Um, you can't do that. This is a crime scene, buddy!"

"What are you gonna do?"

"I know her! I'm taking her to get help!" Robert said, finally standing up. She was heavier than he expected, her coat having taken on a good amount of water. A piece of her wet hair fell in his face. It smelled like oranges. "I'll call the police! I've got her!"

The crowd had a collective feeling of hesitation. Robert could see it in their faces, sense it in their reluctance to move out of the way. But no one said anything. No one stopped him. Someone else was taking care of it. They took one last glance and continued on their way, only slightly late to work now but with a story to share.

Managing to maneuver Piper into a slightly less conspicuous position, Robert trudged through the rain back towards his house. He took the back streets that would be less populated, stopping to catch his breath several times. The fact that no one stopped him or inquired why he was carrying a limp, presumably passed-out woman, made him hate the city even more. He had no plan other than to get her back home and not allow her dead body out of his sight.

With the last of his strength, Robert propped Piper up against his shoulder and unlocked the front door to his house. As he dropped her unceremoniously inside, Jasper came screeching around the corner and stopped at the sight of his drenched owner. Tossing his sopping wet coat to the side, Robert collapsed on the ground next to Piper's crumpled body. The air burned in his lungs as he struggled to inhale and exhale slowly. As he tried to come to terms with what he had just done. Robert took a long breath and looked over at Piper's cold purple hand. He had to try to bring her back.

Robert quickly cleared off the dining room table as papers and dust scattered through the air. With a loud grunt he picked up Piper's body one more time, dropping her on the wood table. He removed her wet jacket and brushed her hair out of her face. Her eyelids were half closed, as though she was glaring at him for his clumsy treatment of her corpse. Robert rolled up his sleeves and took a few steps back.

"I hope this works," he said to her.

It took him a few hours to dig a deep enough hole in the backyard. Robert didn't have enough room available in the tiny corner where the kitten and raccoon had been buried. The only area left was the small plot of green earth that Jasper used for his daily duties. Robert tried to find the cleanest corner of grass and began to dig. Luckily the neighbors on either side of his yard were both at work.

When the hole was done, Robert took one last look around and brought Piper outside. Her body seemed to get heavier and heavier each time he picked her up, as though death was sinking in more and more with each minute that passed. Lowering her into the hole, he took a moment to analyze the grave before covering her up. He wasn't sure how the animals had escaped. He felt a pang of guilt thinking about the creatures having to claw themselves out from underground. If that's how it worked. And he had no idea.

Robert buried Piper up to her collarbone. At least she wouldn't wake up completely underground. Her wilting head kept flopping in awkward angles until he propped it up with a pillow behind the neck. Going inside for a drink of water, Robert and Jasper stared at Piper's exposed head, beyond conspicuous in the open backyard.

"Well, that's not going to work," Robert muttered to Jasper.

With the help of a few garden stakes and a sheet, Robert constructed a haphazard tent that covered the grave. Now it looked as though he had started a garden and protected it with a thick row cover, which was the story he had decided upon if he was asked. He peeked under the sheet at Piper. He had completely closed her eyelids so she appeared to be asleep, nestled in the earth and dreaming of its secrets. He wondered if it was true, if the process had begun, whatever it was and whatever it meant and whatever it did. He wondered if her heart was rustling, quietly thinking of starting again. He went inside and sat on the floor beside the sliding glass door with Jasper, catching glimpses of Piper's sleeping face as the sheet whipped in the wind.

---

Robert glanced at his watch again. He had to leave now if he was going to stop for a latte and still get to work on time. And he sorely needed that latte. The night had been long and uneventful, the little tent in his backyard remaining silent and still as a tomb, Piper locked in her presumably eternal slumber. When the rain started again in the middle of the night, the tent needed the addition of a tarp to keep it waterproof. Finding one in the attic, Robert lumbered in the dim illumination of the back porch light to set it up. Before long, signs of morning inched across the sky, veins of pink and early gold. He and Jasper remained camped by the sliding glass door, watching and waiting.

Stiffly, Robert stood up and changed for work. He ate his breakfast in the kitchen, quietly chewing his cereal while he stared out the window as he had a hundred times before. Outside, Jasper walked gingerly around the tent, mustering the occasional bout of courage to risk a sniff under the sheet before running away. Robert took one last look before leaving Piper for the day. He was leaving a dead body. In his backyard. For an entire day. He went out to adjust the tarp that dipped with gathered rain, pressing down heavily on his makeshift and flimsy white crypt. He checked the stakes one last time, imagining an extra strong gust of wind sweeping into his backyard and revealing Piper's decomposing head for all to see. Finally, he had to leave, ushering Jasper inside the house. The little sentry settled down by the glass door to resume his watch.

"Good boy," Robert said, patting Jasper's head.

He felt a sense of deja vu walking to work that morning, an almost out of body experience as though he was reliving the past but with a new, albeit exhausted, perspective. It was around this same time the morning before that he happened upon Piper's body strewn across the street. But this morning there was no crowd, although he felt a hundred eyes on him all the same. He arrived at the busy coffee shop, now short one experienced barista. Robert joined the line, losing himself within the soft layers of his coat. He closed his eyes and felt himself drifting off, safe and comfortable in its warm embrace.

"Robert."

He opened his eyes and looked into the face of Alex, standing at his side. The detective's face was flat, emotionless. Revealing nothing. It always looked hard, as though he was clenching his jaw so firmly that it was about to crack. Robert had encountered that face in more interviews, interrogations, and meetings than he cared to remember.

"Morning, Detective Shaw," Robert said with a nod, clearing his hoarse throat.

"Morning," Alex replied. He blinked, taking the moment to look Robert up and down. "Everything in order?" he continued, watching Robert's unshaven face very carefully.

Robert cleared his throat again. Alex began to inspect Robert's dirty coat, his eyes studying every detail. A flush began to creep around the edges of Robert's ears as he took quick steps to control his breathing. He had never been a good liar.

"Yes," he answered. "Just have a bit of a head cold, missed work yesterday."

Alex nodded slowly. The line moved up as another patron left and Alex continued along with Robert, his hands clasped in front of his waist.

"That's a shame," Alex said. "Out late?"

"Sorry?"

Alex turned to face Robert directly. He looked straight into Robert's blood shot eyes. "Out in the rain too late?"

The young couple behind Robert and Alex began to snicker, whispering some covert snark. It was enough of a distraction to break Alex's penetrating gaze. Robert sighed heavily and forced himself to smirk.

"Aren't we all out in the rain?" he ventured, trying to make his tone light.

The line moved forward again, bringing Robert closer to his order and eventual escape from the coffee shop and Detective Shaw. His palms began to sweat as he stuffed them into his pockets. Alex worked his jaw back and forth, weighing his next words.

"Say, by the way," he began suddenly. "Do you know that barista that's usually here? Piper?"

Robert hesitated, rather suspiciously he guessed. The fatigue and absence of coffee was making his reactions even slower than usual. He rubbed his stubbly face and shook his head. "No, don't think so."

"Cute, petite one with the red hair? C'mon, I know you've noticed her." Now Alex's tone was dripping with forced levity.

Robert inhaled deeply. "Of course, I've seen her here. I come here a lot. But that's it, I don't know her other than that."

Alex rocked back and forth on his heels and the line finally moved forward another patron. He was nodding to himself, slicking back his tidy hair. The silence that followed was awkwardly long as the two men stood and listened to the next customer's lengthy order.

"You see," Alex switched to a low tone, bordering on a growl. "She's my girlfriend. And I couldn't get in contact with her yesterday. Now, it appears she's missed work this morning." Alex turned to study Robert's heavy coat again, so much that Robert himself looked down as well. There was a dark red strain on the right shoulder, where Piper's head had laid against him.

Robert shrugged, the sweat beginning to gather on the back of his neck. "Sorry to hear that."

Alex attempted to penetrate Robert with his gaze, to sear through his skin and set him on fire. He was standing so close now that Robert could smell his cologne. "And to top it all off, I've been assigned a new case. A murder at Pachelbel's Lizard." Alex was whispering so fiercely that Robert thought he could feel the spittle on his face. He grabbed Robert's arm hard, his hand clamping down through the layers of down. "Been a busy a few days for you, hasn't it, Robert?"

"Morning. What can I get you two?" the barista at the counter interrupted. She looked between the faces of the two men, oblivious to the tense exchange.

Alex released Robert's arm. He smoothed his jacket and looked down at his feet. "Nothing for me, thank you, ma'am. Unfortunately, I'm running late," he said to the barista. He turned his head slightly in Robert's direction. "This line's been a killer."

Brushing past Robert, Alex left Avenue Coffee. The congestion of the crowd fell into a dull blur for Robert, as the barista recognized him and started on the soy latte without another word. Robert pulled his hands out from the warmth of his coat pockets, looking down at the last of the faint ink remaining on his right hand. *A murder at Pachelbel's Lizard.* He closed his eyes and allowed his mind to wander back home, where Jasper was likely still snoozing by the glass door. He wandered further, to his backyard and the white tent flapping in the wind. Wake up, Piper. *Wake up, now.*

# 225 DAYS DEAD

*Dirt. Rain. Blood.* Piper licked her cracked lips and tasted the scent again. It hovered in her nostrils and pressed down on her, damp and suffocating. Dirt, rain, blood, over and over. She heard the faint rustling of branches, scratching and whispering. Her chest felt heavy. Her arms felt very weak, aching at the thought of movement. With great effort, she opened one eye at a time. They felt pasted together with a thick, crusty lining on each lid. The light that broke through caused her to wince, her pupils shouting out with pain. There was white all around her, making the light even more blinding. When her eyes finally conquered the shock and came into focus, Piper found herself level with the ground. Had she fallen? She tried to go back in her memory but all she could recall was darkness. Piper strained to look around herself. She was buried completely beneath the ground, everything except for her head that was awkwardly propped against a pillow.

She sputtered nonsense words as her breath picked up, panicking against the constricting soil around her chest. She tried to move her arms but they were weak and only just regaining sensation. The ground around her was wet and heavy from the rain, a feeling she never thought she would experience. A huge gust of wind ripped against the white tent around her and Piper caught a glimpse of a house with a shining glass door in front of her. She froze. The wind blew by again and she spotted a little dog, watching her with perked up ears. This repeated for several minutes as Piper came to terms with her predicament and surroundings. The little dog became more and more excited, scratching at the glass door and barking. His howling blended in with the whistling of the wind.

Should she scream? *Could she scream?* The air that it would require seemed impossible to conjure at that moment. Piper felt herself starting to slip back into sleep, as though her brain was trying to shut her off from the panic fluttering in her chest. Part of her wanted to return there and part of her wanted to fight. She began to shrug her shoulders, inching them above the cold soil. She gasped as one shoulder finally broke free, allowing room for her chest cavity to expand further. As she continued with this method, the barking from the little dog suddenly became much louder, followed by a scuttling of nails across the cement patio. Piper watched as his wet nose appeared beneath the tent, sniffing left and right. Finally, he burst through with an apparent rush of courage and stared at her, panting.

Piper said nothing, unsure if she even could. The two creatures stared each other down for ten seconds until the dog began to dig. Instinctively, maybe, or just curious to see what would happen if she became free. Either way, it encouraged Piper to keep going, until finally one arm was free and could help with the process. Finally, she removed enough earth to push her weak torso up out of the hole and rolled on to her side, breathing heavily from the exertion.

She laid immobile as the white tent whipped in the wind, providing quick glimpses of her surroundings. Piper could hear the steady rocking of a nearby dock, so she must be near a pier or waterfront. The little dog had retreated outside the tent, pacing back and forth and occasionally sticking his nose beneath the white sheet for a sniff, only to run away again. After several minutes of laying and listening, Piper crawled outside the tent and into the light.

She was in a backyard, a suburban backyard from the looks of it, but not one she was familiar with. It felt like a perfectly normal day, besides having just woke up buried to the neck in dirt. Piper knew she was still in Seattle, the thick gray sky and familiar smells confirmed that for her. The glary sunlight burned her eyes, as though she hadn't seen light for a year and now she was adjusting to its brilliance. She thought she should scream for help, but her throat was so dry she could barely swallow. Crawling across the patio to the ajar glass door, she pushed it open and dropped inside the house, the little dog following right behind her.

Without hesitation, Piper made her way to the kitchen and drank heavily from the sink. She sunk to the floor and looked around the kitchen, noting receipts and flyers stuck to the refrigerator door. The house was silent other than a clock ticking somewhere out of sight. The little dog watched her, poking his head around the corner of the cabinets. The dining room table was cleared off but surrounded by papers and dog treats scattered across the floor. In the corner, Piper found her jacket, damp and stained red with blood. She picked it up and held it in front of her face, hoping to trigger some memory about how she got there.

Looking up, her heavy eyes fell upon a picture mounted on the wall and she met the gaze of Robert and Claire Castle, posed merrily in front of a blurry Christmas tree. Piper's mouth dropped open. She clenched her wet jacket to her chest and looked around the living room closely, leaving a trail of dirt behind her. She went from picture to picture, from trinket to piece of mail, studying it all as she slowly made her way around the house. She peeked out through the closed blinds and saw the familiar street she was on only a few days before. *She was in Robert's house.*

Piper knelt down and looked at the little dog hiding under the table. She beckoned for him and slowly the dog approached, visibly trembling.

"It's okay," Piper whispered hoarsely. She reached out for him, craving to hold something alive and warm. "I think." She flipped over the dog's collar tag. "Hello, Jasper."

Continuing to investigate the house, Piper asked herself numerous times why she wasn't leaving. Why she hadn't already run out the front door like a muddy banshee, screaming for the police. She asked herself why she wasn't on the phone, calling Zelda or even Alex, telling them to come pick her up and bring the troops with them. But here she was, snooping around Robert's house, opening drawers and closets and investigating bottles in the bathroom. It was an opportunity she couldn't pass up, a glimpse into a life she found herself stumbling across again and again. All the while, little Jasper followed her from a safe distance, dropping occasional chew toys at her feet. Piper looked down at the dog, finally noticing the thick amount of mud caked on her shoes. She looked back down the hallway and saw the breadcrumbs of dirt she left on the floor behind her.

Her body hurt. Her stomach felt on the urge of exploding from the amount of sink water she had consumed. Her head pounded with every beat of her heart, as though she could hear the rushing of blood in her ears. Piper entered the master bedroom located at the end of the hall. Jasper sped past her and jumped immediately onto the bed, claiming what was apparently his usual spot. He raised his eyebrows and watched as Piper dropped to the bed without hesitation. The room was so dark and welcoming. The cushiony bed enveloped her, whisking her away from her bodily pain and into a deep, calm sleep. The last thing Piper remembered was her eyes closing and Jasper's steady snore, whispering her to sleep like a soft lullaby.

---

Robert exited Avenue Coffee but did not go to work. He crossed the street and walked in a different direction, towards a music club he had been to a very long time ago. It was in the early days of Robert's courtship with Claire, when they were going out to places to discover each other. They were peeling back layers in public, where it was safe and not so obvious. Claire loved all types of music, and Pachelbel's Lizard was infamous for its eclectic mix of styles. Robert remembered the general location of the club well enough, walking against the crowd at a fast pace. He forgot about work. He even forgot about Piper for a moment. By the time he arrived in front of the closed music club, his soy latte was ice cold. He tossed it aside and walked up to the darkened glass, straining to remember or recognize anything familiar about this place other than what his ancient memories provided. He looked down at his hand and then up at the club's distinct logo of a green lizard. They matched.

The club's door swung open and a tall, balding man carrying a trash can exited the building. He was oblivious to Robert as he hummed and opened the large green dumpster, emptying the contents of his small trash can. Turning back, he jumped and dropped the can with a loud clatter.

"Dude!" the man gasped, bending over to place his hands on his knees as he caught his breath. "I did not see you there, freaking specter, man."

"Sorry," Robert said, holding up his hands.

"Yeah, okay," the man grumbled as he picked up the trash can. He walked back towards the door of Pachelbel's Lizard but stopped, looking back at Robert with squinted eyes.

"You ever find that guy?" the man asked.

"What?"

"From the other night," the man continued. "I remember you."

"You remember me?" Robert's stomach dropped into a cavernous pit. His head began to spin as memories appeared at the edges of his mind. Flashes of faces, loud music, one pungent smell after another. He even began to remember the crunch of the loose gravel on the damp sidewalk. He had been here recently, much more recently than that date with Claire long ago.

"Your jacket, man. You stood out a bit," the man from the club continued, a frown stretching across his stubbly face. "So, you find the guy?"

Robert stammered to find a response, trying to piece together an answer from the brief flashes of information. Struggling with the reality that he had been at this place and had no real recollection of it. The man shook his head and dismissed Robert with a wave.

"Forget it," he sighed heavily. "You know someone got killed here that night, don't you? Crazy place, no night is the same." He turned and began to grumble as he disappeared inside. "Too bad it wasn't that jacket."

The door shut and locked behind the club employee. Robert stared at his reflection in the dark glass, distorted and fragmented. He felt fear. He felt detached from himself, a stranger in his own body. Everything took on a strange aura. A black cat appeared from behind the green dumpster, passing Robert with a cold, green stare. It watched as Robert turned and walked away, his hands in his jacket pockets, his head bent deep in thought. The cat followed him for the long trek back to his house, beneath the swirling sky that threatened rain and all the strangeness that comes with it.

It was early afternoon by the time Robert reached home. He was oblivious to everything, including how many crosswalk signs he violated and how many people he jostled or the black creature following him home. His need to return there was instinctive, his body had enough sense to get him back to a safe place. He could think at home, he could breathe there. It was when Robert reached the front doorstep that he finally snapped into the realization of what waited on the other side.

Jasper sat upright. He sniffed and listened, his ears twitching as he strained to hear as much as possible without having to leave his comfortable spot on the bed. The girl that came out of the ground continued to sleep beside him, occasionally releasing a low snore. He had watched her for a while, sprawled out across the bed, but she hadn't moved a bit. It had actually started to annoy him, this arrangement was not what he was accustomed to. Robert knew exactly how to stretch his legs to leave Jasper the optimal amount of room. Just as he was settling down again, Jasper heard the familiar click of the front door unlocking. He used Piper as a spring board and launched himself off the bed, racing down the hallway and greeting Robert just as he opened the door.

Robert quickly closed the door behind him. He shushed Jasper's excited yelps and froze when he saw the sliding glass door wide open. Running to the backyard, Robert whipped open the white tent and dropped to his knees when he found the open grave. He fingered the loose soil, shoveling more aside as though Piper could have sunk deeper beneath the earth. He turned as Jasper began barking in a high-pitched tirade, howling at the black cat that was watching from the fence line. Robert left Jasper to harass the feline, focused on the trail of dirt clods that led into the house. He followed it to the kitchen, down the hallway, until reaching his bedroom doorway. Piper was passed out in his bed, her arms draped over her head as though trying to block out all light. He inched closer, holding his breath until he saw her chest expand with a long, deep inhalation of life returned.

Quietly stepping backwards, Robert exited his bedroom and shut the door, leaving it slightly cracked. He took one last look until shuffling down the hallway, wondering if this was all real. If any of this was real. But then Jasper returned to the house, lapping at his bowl of water in between pants. Then he saw the familiar stacks of dishes and the bag of trash he meant to take out days ago. Everything was real, it was happening, a woman was dead and now she's back to life and he had played a part in it. Robert stood by the sink and gripped the counter hard. He was spinning. He was in a whirlwind that was carrying him away at an uncontrollable speed, hurling him into territory ruled by impossibilities. Robert reached out for the coffee pot, the lid rattling as he struggled to steady his shaking hand. This is what Claire would have done. She always knew she could calm his nerves with a pot of thick coffee.

*Claire.* Robert watched the black tears drop down into the hot pot. He jingled the keys in his pocket, the sound building into a tangled melody. He looked up at the impending evening through the kitchen window. If he left now, maybe he could get there in time. He knew the graveyard closed for visitors at 8:00 pm, turning off all the street lights for reinforcement. But Robert could have found his way to Claire's grave with his eyes and ears covered. His heart began to pound against his chest like a war cry, he felt thick urgency in his throat thinking about his dead wife beneath layers and layers of earth. He could bring her back. *He could bring her back.* The coffee pot sizzled with one final exhale of black gold, settling into silence as the phone rang.

"Yes?" Robert picked it up on the first ring.

It was met by silence, followed by a few muffled sniffles.

"Bobby?" a voice finally whispered.

"Grant?"

"I'm glad you answered."

"What's going on?"

"The baby didn't make it," Grant choked. He wept for a few seconds before adding quietly, "It's brutal."

"No," Robert sighed, bending down to lean his forehead on the cold counter. "I'm sorry."

"I don't know what we're going to do. Everything was about…" Grant sobbed.

Robert just listened. No words of his were going to help right now. Outside, the sky had turned completely dark but the white tent glowed beneath the slim moonlight. Jasper was hiding under the table, staring down the hallway with wide eyes. Robert turned at the sound of slow shuffling across the floors as Piper appeared in the kitchen, her eyelids heavy and swollen. Her clothes were stained with dirt and blood, her hair was dusty brown and clumped with grass and sweat. She said nothing, her eyes moving from Robert to the coffee pot as she licked her dry lips.

"Grant," Robert interrupted. He fumbled for a nearby coffee cup and filled it, offering the mug to Piper. Her eyes lingered on the cup until finally reaching out and accepting it. She took a long drink, watching Robert over the edge of the cup.

"What?" Grant mumbled.

"Are you having a funeral?" Robert asked, his eyes locked on Piper. She seemed fuzzy, as if in a daze. But she was living. She was breathing. She was back. His heart pounded so hard he felt close to exploding.

"Yes. Yes, we will."

"When?" Robert turned to look out the window but only saw his reflection staring back. Watching and listening for what he was going to do next.

"I don't know. I don't know, soon," Grant stammered.

"Make sure you let me know. I want to help."

Robert hung up. He waited a few beats before turning back to Piper. She was still staring at him from behind her coffee cup, as though it was a shield. Her eyes did not communicate fear. They communicated nothing. Robert poured himself his own mug of coffee and cleared his throat, watching her through the steam. She was back, but was she *she?* Finally, Piper lowered her cup and Robert could see her visibly trying to swallow. It took a few moments for her to regain command of her tongue before managing a few scratchy words.

"You'll need to wash your sheets."

# 228 DAYS DEAD

Piper added another blanket to the growing pile already atop her. She glanced at the digital clock across the dark room. *2:43 am.* She never stayed up this late, ever. She had worked since she was a teenager and learned quickly that a body without sleep did not function well. But that had changed since the accident. Piper had started calling it *the accident*, not only for her own sanity, but so she wouldn't slip and tell someone she had been brought back from the dead. She hadn't left her apartment since Robert dropped her off a few days before. As far as work or her friends or Alex knew, Piper had fallen and twisted her ankle and needed to rest up. But truly, Piper needed a few days to process that she had literally swam back across the River Styx.

She didn't have much to ponder. She had no memory of being hit by a car, of dying, of death, the afterlife, or anything that happened up until she opened her eyes beneath the big, bright white tent. Robert offered as much information as he had, which wasn't much. He had pieced together a strange recipe of steps he identified as necessary to bring the dead back to life. But really he was flailing, he was riding a dangerous wave that was growing into an out of control tsunami. And he had found Piper floating in the water and dragged her along with him. She wasn't mad. She wasn't anything. She felt no different other than a restlessness that kept her up late into the night, always ravenous and usually cold. She spent this time watching late night shows, fascinated by their content and strangely comforted at the idea there were others out there, up late and accompanied by their television set, just like her. Or maybe not completely like her.

Tossing the empty cracker box to the ground, Piper picked up the remote and began to sift through shows. She searched beneath the blankets for any remaining boxes of snacks. There were a few more minutes left to her favorite cooking show rerun and Piper was determined to go to bed at 3:00 am, no later. A commercial flickered across the screen and an obnoxiously loud announcer began to speak over a flashing graphic.

"Unsure about your love life? Wondering if you're up for that promotion? Worried about the future? Are you just looking for answers? We have them at Our Nation's Psychic Network! Call and speak to one of our seasoned and professional psychics now!"

Piper stopped looking for more food and watched the screen.

A sad-looking woman dressed in an oversized bathrobe and plastic shower cap appeared on screen. "My husband started working late and I just didn't trust him. Was he having an affair? Then I called Our Nation's Psychic Network and found out the truth."

Next, a man dressed in a construction uniform popped onto the screen. He solemnly removed his helmet and began to speak. "I needed direction. I needed real answers, ones that my family and friends couldn't help me with. I called Our Nation's Psychic Network and got the confidential help I needed."

Piper reached for her cell phone as a distinguished man in a suit appeared over a background of swirling stars.

"That's right, you can get help today. Just call the number below and we'll connect with you with one of our discreet psychics. What are you waiting for? *$2.99 a minute plus applicable fees and taxes. See website for full details.*"

Without pause, Piper punched in the phone number that flashed across the television screen and was immediately met by dreamy hold music. She had never called a 900 number, and in fact, didn't know they still existed. Maybe they only remained in this strange limbo that was not quite night and not quite morning, a time where people should be sleeping but instead were up late eating.

A few clicks and disclaimer messages later, Piper was finally connected to a member of Our Nation's Psychic Network.

"Hi," a woman's deep voice whispered over the line. "Who am I speaking with today?"

"Um, hello," Piper stammered. "I'm Piper." She wondered if she should give a fake name but it was too late now. "Yeah, Piper."

"Piper," the voice repeated. "What answers can I help you seek?"

"I'm not sure."

The woman seemed to stifle a sigh. "We all get a little lost sometimes. Let's see if I can help. How's your love life?"

"I don't care about that right now."

"Are you contemplating any job changes?"

"No. I like my job."

The psychic cleared her throat. "Family problems?"

"They're dead."

"So you want to get in contact with them?"

"No, not really."

The phone went silent for a few beats. "Do you just need someone to talk to? If you're thinking of hurting yourself, I can refer you to…"

"No, no," Piper interrupted. "This is totally confidential, right?"

"Well, I do encourage you to visit the website for full details."

"I just want you to look into my future and tell me what you see," Piper insisted.

The psychic fell silent. Piper wondered if the woman had given up on her until she heard a long, drawn out sigh.

"Did you hear what I said?"

"One moment, please," the psychic replied firmly.

Piper checked the clock. It was now 3:08 am. She didn't want to think about how quickly that $2.99 a minute was stacking up to a fat phone bill. The woman on the other line cleared her throat and sighed again.

"Are you suffering from an illness?" she finally asked.

"I really don't want any more questions. I just want to know what you see in my future. Just tell me frankly, I can handle it. Trust me."

The psychic cleared her throat again. "I don't see anything."

Piper stopped mid-bite on a chip she found on the couch. "Nothing?" she repeated.

"It's a unique situation," the psychic continued, her voice now changing from mysterious to curious. "We all have paths. Maybe not so clear, but some sort of path has been laid out for us all in the cosmos. But for you, there's nothing."

"I have no path? What the heck does that mean?"

"As though there's nothing planned for you. You are unknown to the cosmos."

"What? Is that good? Or bad?"

"That is for you to determine, Piper," the psychic replied, her voice turning back to a mysterious whisper. "I hope you choose wisely. Is there anything else I can answer for you?"

Piper ended the call and tossed her phone onto the ground. Either she had no path in the cosmos or that psychic was truly perplexed on how to advise her. Maybe her original path had ended when that car struck her and the new path never picked up again. She looked around at the piles of blankets and empty boxes of food. Her skin began to crawl. She wasn't truly supposed to be here. She was supposed to be dead. Maybe she was flying under the radar of the cosmos, cutting her way through the swirling stars and planets. Maybe she'd discover something new. Or maybe she'd fall into a black hole and never come out again.

These thoughts were leading her into a heavy sleep, holding her hand as they dragged her deeper and deeper into slumber. Piper jumped a beat before the pounding on her door officially roused her back to consciousness. She looked at the clock. It was 3:33 am. No one should be knocking at her door at 3:33 am. Carefully cracking her curtain, Piper peeked out the window and saw Robert standing on her front patio, his expression wide-eyed and wild.

He burst in as soon as Piper turned the door knob, spraying her with rain droplets that had gathered on Robert's soaked coat. She looked down at the track of mud left in his wake as he paced around her apartment, entering the kitchen and opening cupboard after cupboard.

"Water," he panted, motioning around the room. "Can I have some water, please."

Piper said nothing as she poured him a glass of water that Robert immediately guzzled. She started pouring him another as she watched Robert visibly try to calm himself. He was drenched from hair to shoes, his jeans caked with mud and other debris. His eyes were flickering from corner to corner, as though trying to keep up with the rapid fire of thoughts snapping through his mind. Finally getting his breath in check, he focused carefully on his next words, fixated on his outstretched hand. "It didn't work."

Shifting her weight, Piper kept her gaze on Robert and shook her head. She was having to put effort into keeping her eyelids up.

"Claire," Robert said. "I tried to bring back Claire and it didn't work."

He watched Piper's reaction desperately, as though it was going to give him guidance on where to turn or what to do next. Piper felt her face fall flat as she processed what Robert had said. She began to rummage around the kitchen, motioning for Robert to go sit in the living room.

"I need chocolate," she mumbled, digging through drawers and cabinets until finally unearthing a half-eaten bag of chocolate morsels. She joined Robert on the couch, plopping onto the pile of blankets. "Start from the beginning."

Robert took a deep breath and looked over his shoulder at the front door. He removed his wet coat and tossed it to the ground, running his muddy hands through his hair. "I couldn't wait," he admitted, shaking his head. "I couldn't wait another minute without trying to bring her back."

"So you went to her grave," Piper urged, wanting to say the words for him.

"Yes," Robert whispered. He was disintegrating and slipping away with every passing second. "I waited until it was dark. It takes a long time to dig that deep. I didn't know she would look like that." He looked over at Piper miserably. "She almost looked the same, in a way."

Piper swallowed hard. She wouldn't have known what to expect, either.

"I tried to hold her," Robert continued, clenching his fists. "I tried to imagine her alive again. But nothing. Nothing happened. I don't know why."

"I'm sorry," Piper whispered, reaching out to touch his shoulder. "I'm so sorry."

"I took her," Robert added quickly.

"What."

"I took Claire," Robert repeated. He pointed towards the front door. "She's in the car."

Piper put down the chocolate. She was wide awake now.

Robert started pacing again, leaving tracks on the carpet. He began repeating the story, as though he was trying to process the evening all over again. "I filled in the grave. Put the tools back in the trunk. But I couldn't leave her there." He turned to Piper. "I couldn't put her back."

"No, no," Piper said. Her mind snapped into action as she grabbed Robert's muddy arms. "You need to go home. Put Claire somewhere safe while it's still dark out. Is the backyard still setup?"

Robert nodded.

"Okay. That's good. Bury her there until we figure something out."

Robert reached down to pick up his coat. He stared at it, studying it, lost in its layers. He turned to Piper, a small flicker of relief visible in his eyes.

She walked with him to the door. "Are you working tomorrow?" she asked.

"No."

"I'm back at work tomorrow. I'll come by your house after my shift."

Robert replaced his coat and feeling its dampness, immediately removed it. He fumbled on the doorstep, his shaking hands jingling his keys. He was looking down at his car and the lifeless form that was wrapped up tightly within in. Turning to Piper, Robert's eyes were black, masked beneath long shadows caused by the flickering light overhead.

"Thank you," he whispered.

Piper shook her head. "I owe you one."

---

Walking across the precarious stepping stones to the front door, Piper's instinct was to begin digging for a key in her purse, as though Robert's house was her home as well. She ended and began there, it felt strange to Piper to knock on the front door like a common visitor. Moments later, she heard the scuttle of little toenails and imagined Jasper rounding the corner and sliding to a stop at the front door. She knocked again. There was no answer other than Jasper's muffled whines. Glancing over her shoulder, Piper saw no one else out on that drizzly afternoon. She had come here straight after work, even taking a bus to hasten the voyage. She felt distracted all day, getting orders wrong and clumsily deflecting Zelda's questions. Avenue Coffee was the last place she needed to be.

Easing her way behind the row of thick Rhododendrons that lined the front of the house, Piper made her way to the side gate and jiggled it. Locked. This sound prompted a warning bark from Jasper that still did not rouse any further activity in the house. Tossing her bag over the locked gate, Piper summoned every last bit of agility and hoisted herself up and over. She landed on the wet concrete and was met by the stare of a black cat, spread out leisurely and mid-lick on one of its paws.

Piper exclaimed breathlessly. "Scared me, you creepy thing," she whispered, standing up and grabbing her bag.

The cat stared at her an extra beat then returned to licking its paw.

Piper's stomach dropped when she rounded the corner and stepped into the backyard. She was overwhelmed with a wash of memories, the gripping panic of waking up mostly underground. The sound of the tent flapping in the wind reminded her of the wings of a great bird, circling the backyard and preparing to swoop down with the gift of life when the time was right. Walking up to the tent, Piper took a long breath and reached out to open it.

The sliding glass door slid open and Jasper burst out into the backyard, speeding past Piper and in the direction of the black cat. Robert was standing in the doorway, his hair sticking up in sweaty crags and his face hanging long like an avalanche. He was still dressed in the muddy clothes from the night before, down to his socks and shoes. He stared at the white tent, barely aware of Piper as he rushed over, glanced inside, then shut the tent again solemnly.

"You look horrible," Piper stated, looking Robert up and down. "Really, really horrible."

"Coffee?" Robert croaked, motioning for Piper to follow him inside.

"What happened last night?" Piper continued. "Did anything…change?"

Robert shook his head, going through the motions at the coffeemaker. He didn't speak until he saw evidence of the coffee brewing, slow drips accumulating one by one.

"I came here," he sighed, rubbing his head hard. "I got her into the backyard the best I could. Jasper was a mess." Robert rubbed his head harder and harder, as though trying to conjure up memories from the night before. "Then I…then I…" he mumbled, turning to the coffeemaker. He mouthed the words so quietly that Piper leaned in to hear them.

"What?" she whispered.

"I don't know," Robert repeated, staring at the wall. Turning to Piper, his face was panicked. "I really don't know."

"You probably just went to bed," Piper said. "You're still wearing your shoes, you probably just collapsed. I mean, you did just dig up your dead wife. Slightly traumatizing."

Robert shook his head, looking down at his filthy shoes. He rushed into the living room, digging through couch cushions.

"What time is it?" he asked, moving onto the coffee table cluttered with paperwork.

"Almost five," Piper answered, helping herself to a cup of coffee. She continued under her breath, "Too late for this but who cares anymore."

Finally locating the remote control, Robert fumbled with the buttons until turning to the news. He sat down onto the couch rigidly and Piper joined him, glancing occasionally at his frozen expression. The highlights of the evening's newscast appeared onscreen.

"A murder that took place in Mercer Island early this morning is being called calculated and clean by investigators," the newscaster read into the screen. "It was a grisly scene for morning jogger Pamela Rose, who came across the deceased body on the route of her usual run. No further details have been released other than it is still an ongoing investigation."

Video of a distraught woman with wet hair speaking to a reporter came across the television. Close-ups of crime scene tape and well-dressed detectives followed.

"Hey, it's Alex!" Piper shouted, pointing at the screen. Footage of Alex gathered with other detectives played for only a few seconds, but she could recognize his shiny mountain of hair anywhere.

"Detectives are asking that anyone with information in connection to the case should call their hotline immediately."

Robert slung the remote control across the room and stalked to the front door. He picked up his jacket from the ground, rummaging through the pockets and shaking the garment upside down. Finding nothing, Robert reached into his jeans pockets and began dumping change and other trash onto the coffee table in front of Piper. She watched him from across the rim of her cup of coffee as he inspected each receipt and straw wrapper. Finally, he found a bus ticket stub that caused him to pause. His eyes ran over the information several times, changing speed as he methodically read each word.

"What?" Piper asked, leaning closer.

As Robert turned the receipt towards Piper, she squinted to read the smeared ink.

"It's a ticket to Mercer Island," he explained, holding the ticket so tightly that it began to crumple beneath his touch. Piper snatched the ticket and inspected it for herself as Robert collapsed to the ground. "From late last night."

"After you left my apartment," Piper said. "What, are you saying you don't remember?"

Robert's face turned sallow. "No. Just like Pachelbel's Lizard," he murmured, rubbing his hand where the stamp had been.

"You don't remember that?" Piper repeated.

Robert's face snapped up. Piper dropped the ticket and raised her hands before explaining. "I was there with my friend, we saw you leave Pachelbel's Lizard. It was the night they had a murder there. Or, a recent murder I should say, that place is a mess. Anyway, we kind of followed you for a bit. Okay, we followed you all the way back here."

Robert shook his head, his hand reaching out for the ticket. He fingered his filthy clothes, studying the cracks and creases of his worn hands. He leaned down and cradled his head. He whispered a few words to himself before Jasper appeared and climbed into his owner's lap and they melded together.

Piper's stomach began to twist. "You think you had something to do with those murders?" She shook her head. "That's crazy."

"Crazier than bringing the dead back to life?" Robert asked. He stood up and Jasper stayed close behind. "I think...I think I have done this other times as well. I've woken up like this before. I thought it was fatigue. I thought it was grief," he stammered. He turned to Piper, his face contorted. "I can't be trusted. You should leave."

Piper jumped up and stood next to Robert. She wanted to place her hand on Robert's arm. It looked tense, locked up in terror. "I do trust you," she whispered. "If you did have something to do with those killings, maybe there was a reason."

"A reason?" Robert exclaimed as he walked away from her. "No. No, there is never a reason for taking a life," he said loudly, beginning to pace the floor. "I'll need to be tracked. I can't trust that I'll stay here at the house. I need to be watched." He looked down at Jasper then they both looked over at Piper. "Stay with me," Robert pleaded, grabbing Piper's hand. "Watch me. Slap me out of it. Stop me from taking one more life." He let go of Piper and leaned against the countertop, cradling his head. "Kill me if you have to," he whispered.

Piper studied Robert's crumpled form. "I'll stay," she agreed, patting him on the back. She was beginning to see where she fit into this colossal puzzle. He looked over his shoulder at her, eyes slightly swollen. "I'll stay with you."

A particularly sharp wind passed through the backyard, causing the tent to flap loudly and reach high into the sky, a pillar of white flashing by like a skyrocketing ghost. The black cat watched and waited, lounging beneath the fluttering tent, guarding its prized possession buried in the backyard.

# 231 DAYS DEAD

Funerals brought back too many memories. From the early loss of Robert's father, a death that happened while he was very young, to his mother's passing several years ago, her beloved church filled with the aroma of freshly-cut roses. And finally Claire's funeral, where Robert stood on the edge of her grave, ready to jump in after her. He was still a suspected man at that point, wincing through the cautious sympathies. He remembered the wary pats on the shoulder delivered by friends and family, unsure if they were consoling a cold murderer or a grieving widower. Robert had waited until the last shovelful of dirt rested atop her grave and for hours after, just in case she called for him from the depths below. Just in case, he would be there. Now here he was, at another funeral. Grant looked over his shoulder at Robert and nodded. He wiped his eyes with his large rough hands and looked back to the grave. Maybe he was listening for a call beneath the soil, too.

Standing several feet behind Grant and Shannon, Robert stared at their hunched over shoulders. Grant wrapped his arm around Shannon but he couldn't stop his hand from shaking. He gripped it over and over but the trembling was still visible. This was their child's funeral. This was something they should have never seen. Robert pushed his hands into his suit pockets and looked over his shoulder at Piper, who watched the funeral from a distance. She was a statue of black in her long skirt and matching blouse, concealed conspicuously next to a nearby tree.

Piper had travelled the miles to join Robert at the infant's funeral. She didn't question or balk at it, instead calling in sick to work. The last few days had been a whirlwind of adjustments. Robert and Jasper had not shared their house with another human being in too long, much less a high maintenance one that demanded a good amount of time in the bathroom. But he couldn't complain, when Robert's head hit the pillow at night he was grateful to know Piper's presence was around the corner. At work, they kept track of each other with texts and calls. But Robert wasn't worried about the day. He was worried about those hours between final consciousness and morning. Nothing good ever happened after 2:00 am.

Once the ceremony was over, the small crowd began to disperse. Robert wouldn't leave, he wouldn't move until Grant and Shannon were safely back in their car. Their roles had been switched almost a year ago and they hadn't moved, either. Once the funeral party left the graveyard to travel to the wake, Robert remained and hovered several feet from the small, open grave. His pulse jumped. He had given this afternoon hours of thought, dreaming of the possibility he hadn't lost it. That maybe the failure with Claire, who remained safely nestled in the backyard beneath Jasper's watchful gaze, had been a fluke. That maybe a recent loss of life was easier to bring back than the stale, as though the hope of reawakening lingered briefly beneath the skin like synapses waiting to be reignited. Robert stepped closer to the edge, the tip of his shoe sticking out over the expanse. His heart beat harder, faster, until Robert had to take a breath to calm himself. It was then that he felt a second pulsing, separate from his own, in the tip of his index finger.

With the crowd completely gone, Piper joined Robert at the graveside. She sighed and exhaled loudly. "This sucks."

"I can do it," Robert announced, holding up his index finger. His eyes were wide and alert. "I feel her."

Piper raised an eyebrow and focused on Robert's finger. "There?" she asked. In the last few days, Piper had received a crash course on Robert's communications quirks. Her only method for survival was constant clarification.

"We need to get to the wake," Robert said as he turned on his heel and started trudging towards his car.

"I thought you weren't going to do this," Piper reminded, struggling to keep up with Robert's pace. "If it doesn't work, I mean…it's their kid, Robert."

Robert fumbled with his keys until realizing the car was unlocked. He started the ignition, holding his finger out precariously as though afraid to break whatever connection had been established. He looked over at Piper, who was standing in the road, not moving.

"Let's go," he nudged.

"What are you going to do?" she demanded.

"I'm going to talk to Grant and Shannon."

"And tell them what? That you want to try to bring back their dead baby?"

Robert paused and turned to stare at the steering wheel. "Something like that."

"First," Piper said, taking a deep breath. "You've got horrible timing. Second, can you safely expose yourself to these people? Third, what if it doesn't work?"

"But what if it does," Robert said. He held out his finger to Piper.

Piper stared at it. "That's not going to convince me."

Robert didn't move, his hand unwavering, silent other than the steady ticking of his car's engine. Finally, Piper stepped forward and wrapped her fingers around Robert's. It was a few seconds before she felt the first beat, slow and faint. Seconds later, another sluggish beat. And another. It couldn't have been Robert's heartbeat. But if not his, then whose?

At the wake, the air in the house was stuffy from the confined space being filled with too many warm bodies. The wake had been arranged by Grant and Shannon's church, the food a representation of the many different tastes that attended there. As afternoon faded into night, Robert watched Grant remain a silent companion forever present at Shannon's side, resigned to eat blandly from his plate of cheese and crackers and receive embrace after embrace. He never met Robert's gaze but Robert could see the gears turning and creaking in his friend's mind. Mourner after mourner left the house until only a few stragglers remained, close relatives that were afraid to release the young couple into the abyss of grief on their own.

Piper stayed with Robert, playing off she was a friend of Grant and Shannon's. She walked around their house and studied the pictures and art and began to form an idea about the couple. She watched as Shannon crumpled at the approach of yet another condolence and how Grant flexed his jaw repeatedly. She felt the weight of the empty void upstairs, the nursery door firmly shut, displaying the name *Abby*.

"Now?" Piper suggested beneath her breath.

Robert surveyed the room. Shannon was preoccupied with her sister, her head resting against the cold folding chair. Grant stood by the refreshments and poured himself yet another cup of coffee, spilling droplets on the white tablecloth. He brushed at the spots several times before giving up and downing the beverage.

Robert's palms began to sweat as he approached Grant. "I'm so sorry," he stammered.

Grant turned to Robert and nodded, exhaling loudly. "I know, man. Thank you."

"And I want to help," Robert continued, meeting Piper's gaze from across the room. She was watching closely, as though trying to read Robert's lips.

"You making the trip out here, that was awesome of you. That's enough right there," Grant said through sips of more coffee.

"I can do more. Or, I believe I can, anyway."

Grant shook his head. "You are a good friend, man, I appreciate you."

*I can bring your baby back*, Robert thought to himself. He clenched his fists over and over. Maybe if he thought it first, he would find a way to say it. "I can bring her back."

Grant lowered his cup. Robert heard Piper hold her breath.

"What did you say?" Grant asked in a low voice, leaning closer.

The pulse in Robert's finger surged. *Don't give up. Don't give up, now.*

"I can bring your baby back to life," Robert stated, straightening his shoulders.

Grant looked dazed. "You mean this in some spiritual way, man? You never seemed like, I don't know, into that."

"Grant," Robert started again. He gripped his friend's shoulders firmly. "We can go to the graveyard and bring Abby back alive."

Robert watched his friend's face turn a slightly purple shade of red. He expected a reaction like this and tensed at the possibility of a punch to the gut. Grant's face trembled as tears bubbled to the surface. "What the hell is wrong with you, Bobby?"

Grant began to walk off but Robert grabbed his arm firmly. "I can do it!" he whispered.

Yanking his arm away, Grant pointed a finger in Robert's face, inches from contact. "That is the sickest thing you could have ever said to me. Ever."

"I can do it," Robert insisted levelly, stepping closer as he waved away Grant's hand and lowered his voice. "Trust me."

The interaction drew the attention of the remaining members of the room. Grant turned away to comfort Shannon, whose pale face looked close to shattering. He helped his wife stand up and ushered her towards the stairs, shooting Robert daggers as he escorted Shannon upstairs step by step. Robert didn't look away. *Don't give up.*

An hour passed and everyone else left. Piper cleaned the best she could in a stranger's house, quietly finding her way around the kitchen as she searched for trash bags and foil. Robert waited at the base of the stairs, hearing the soft footsteps of Grant and Shannon. He would wait here all night. All day. All year. *Don't give up.* Right now he was a messenger, a sentry for the dead, and he would not leave until he was heard.

Grant appeared in the hallway. He was faltering, Robert could see it in his eyes even from the distance. There was a flicker of doubt there, a crazy thought racing across his mind, fueled by grief and fatigue. He walked across the hall and paused at the nursery door. There was a nightstand outside the door with a lamp set to dim, a little flame of hope in the long passage of night. Grant descended the staircase and stopped inches from Robert's face.

"Is this what you told me about before? The animals?" Grant asked.

"Yes."

"How?"

"I don't know exactly. But I have a sort of a pattern from the times before," Robert answered. He looked up as Piper entered from the kitchen, wiping her damp hands on her shirt.

Grant looked at her, raising an eyebrow. "Is this…?"

"I'm Piper." She waved her hand slightly, unsure what else to do. "Yep, I'm one of the times before."

---

The two men stood over the fresh grave. Piper hung back but at a watchable distance. The details of the soil were still crisp, even in the bare light of the waning moon. The smell of the freshly turned dirt was pungent. Layers once hidden were now excavated to the surface, releasing the petrichor of a thousand miniscule creatures set free. Robert thought he could hear them squirming, invigorated by the change. He looked over at Grant in the fuzzy darkness, waiting for some sort of signal that he was ready.

Grant turned on his flashlight, its beam piercing the thick darkness of the empty cemetery. He had never looked so weak and small to Robert. The trip back to the graveyard had been a rushed ride of blurry questions that had no real answer other than Robert asking for Grant's trust. A blind trust, hanging by thin beats of life.

"Bobby," he whispered. "I have one more thing to ask you."

"Go ahead."

"What will she come back as?" Grant choked. He began to

sob, trying to fight through the words. "I know I didn't know her. But will she come back as someone different?"

Robert hadn't considered this. He suddenly feared he had no idea what he was doing. He had not thought to question if Piper would be different. He was on a rollercoaster of acting and reacting.

"They're alive. That's what's different," Robert said finally.

With a deep inhale and exhale, Grant composed himself. He nodded and plunged his shovel into the soil. He began to dig wildly, scraping away the fresh dirt with breathless urgency. Robert attempted to keep up, moving out of the way once Grant reached the tiny coffin. The visual was shocking, an eerie outline in the darkness. Grant froze, staring down at the tiny wooden box. He climbed out of the hole and stood next to Robert, his tear-streaked face illuminated by the flashlight.

"What's next?" he asked.

Robert swallowed hard. He ran his muddy fingers through his hair. "We're going to have to open it up. I need to touch her. Then, we'll bury her again. I guess we'll need to bury you, you can hold her."

Grant handed the shovel to Robert and turned away. He met Piper's gaze from where she knelt a few feet away, her face overcome with emotion. He listened to Robert drop into the grave, shuddering at the sound of wood cracking open, the hiss of confined air breaking free, the muffled sounds of Piper crying into her hands. His stomach turned as he smelled the faint odor that had plagued his memories for the last week. It was the odor of death and chemicals colliding. He had a momentary flutter of nerves, terrified to think what the small form of his infant daughter had become. He heard the soft shuffle of fabric. The scratching of shoes against the exterior of the coffin. Then Robert cleared his throat behind him.

"Grant," he whispered. "Now."

Eyes diverted, Grant climbed down into the grave. He took the weightless form in his arms, glancing quickly enough to see that Robert had wrapped her discreetly in the soft blanket from her coffin. He sat down in the grave and closed his eyes as

Robert filled the grave again with soil up to Grant's elbows.

"How long, Bobby?" Grant whispered, his voice weak. He became very aware of the sounds around him. The rustling of the leaves in the wind. The faraway rush of the freeway traffic. The coldness of the soil soaked through his clothes, welcoming him to its dark depths.

"I don't know, it seems to vary," Robert sighed, settling down at the edge of the grave. "But I'm not leaving until she wakes up."

Hours passed. Robert kept watch on the still form wrapped in his friend's trembling arms, counting the steady beats on the tip of his finger. Piper eventually joined him by his side after composing herself, overwhelmed by watching the process from this side of the soil. Grant passed in and out of consciousness, the position of his arm never changing as he kept his child suspended in the sea of soil.

Robert thought about Shannon's wilted body sleeping fitfully back at her home, lost amidst the blankets. It reminded him too much of Claire, drowning in the loss of yet another pregnancy. Robert pushed himself to not blink. He willed Grant's daughter to awake over and over again in his mind, imagining what her cry would sound like in that quiet night air. He thought ahead to the future, picturing Grant and Shannon's life with their child back again. And when the first lines of dawn finally appeared on the horizon, Robert felt the pulse in his finger halt as returned life took a breath.

# 235 DAYS DEAD

Robert stood in the doorway, listening. The cries he had imagined in his mind were now real sounds. His skin went cold at the accuracy of it. It was a croupy cough, as though the tiny infant was hacking up old pieces of lung to be replaced by the new. She was with Shannon, who awoke to find her baby on the bed next to her, squirming and alive. Shannon had asked no questions, as though this had all been a dream and she was finally awake. Grant leaned against the door frame, face drained of all color besides the stain of brown mud on his face. His mouth hung, his heavy shoulders weighed down by exhaustion. He rubbed the coarse stubble on his jaw and shook his head, trying several times to start a sentence.

"How is this real?" he finally whispered.

Robert balled up his wrinkled suit coat and patted his friend on the shoulder. He was beyond asking himself that same question. The experience fades into a blur, a spinning world of hands and tears and darkness. The smell of death mixed with soil and the spark of reignited life. How was any of it real.

"I won't tell anyone, Bobby. I swear it." Grant swirled around to grip Robert's shoulders. His eyes looked wild. "We'll leave town, no one will know."

"I know, I know. We'll talk later, just enjoy having her back," Robert said, his voice dry and crackly. He wanted to get home and check on Claire. And then to sleep for hours and hours. He felt drained, to a level beyond fatigue. Turning to leave down the hallway, he took one last look at the new family, finally complete. They were outlines against the dawn, new forms ready to take on the awaiting day.

Outside, rain had started. A hot rain, drawing gentle lines in the dust on the car's windshield. Piper had been asleep since they arrived safely back at Grant's house, sprawled across the backseat, her eyes pressed shut tightly as though warding off any distraction that might rouse her. Robert started the car and sat silent, watching the wipers move across the windshield back and forth. Back and forth. Upstairs in Grant's house, a light turned on and then another. Robert watched the figures move within. He had done that. He had made that happen. He clenched his filthy hands around the steering wheel until he thought his knuckles would burst. Why had it worked for them, but not for him? Why that child or Piper or a bug, but not Claire?

Robert drove home in a blur and in an instant, he was back. As he gathered his coat, he could already hear Jasper's barks from inside, likely out of food and water and covered in mud from the new rain. Later, he would blame it on the fatigue, but he never saw the figures come to surround his car until the loud tapping of a flashlight on his window drew his attention. Alex peered down at Robert through the streams of rain, a look of triumph and disgust across his face. His gaze drifted to Piper's sleeping form curled up in the backseat and in an instant the door was yanked open and Robert was on the ground.

"What did you do to her?" Alex screamed into Robert's ear as he pressed his knees into Robert's back, removing a pair of handcuffs from his belt.

Robert couldn't have answered if he wanted to, unable to breathe until Alex finally stood up. Beyond the ringing in his ears he could hear Piper's shouts and Jasper's high pitched howling from behind the backyard fence. The world finally came to a spinning stop as he was slammed against the hood of his car and a dozen faces came into focus. Seattle police officers. He felt his stomach turn sour. He had been here before. He craned his head to look at back at Piper, who was shouting at Alex several feet away.

"Let him go!" Piper slurred, still waking from her heavy sleep. She reached out to give Alex a sluggish shove, which he easily avoided.

"Have you been drugged?" Alex held Piper's shoulders, peering down into her line of sight. "How long has he had you?"

This time Piper's shove landed. The other officers visibly held back chuckles. Jasper's barking escalated to a new level of frenzy and neighbors began to poke out from their front doors. "I don't respond to your text messages so now I've been kidnapped, is that it? Grow up!" she shouted. "I've been working with him. And you have no right to be here right now!"

Alex stared at Piper for a few beats, slicked back his hair then turned without a word, drawing an envelope from his coat pocket. He held it in Robert's line of sight, ink smearing in the relentless, hot rain.

"See you back at the station, old sport," he said.

---

It was the same style of table. Or maybe even the very same one. Maybe he was even in the very same room as his first interrogation, where Robert's shaking hands had spilled coffee all over the scuffed folding table. Beyond the closed door, the sounds of the police station buzzed and rang, a commotion of voices and boot scratches. The recycled and stale air reeked of coffee and metal. But the confusion that scrambled Robert the first time was not there now. Now, he understood why.

Alex seemed to notice. He tapped his pen rhythmically against the metal table, a thudding pang over and over. His dark eyes searched every corner of Robert's face, his hair still glistening from the rain storm.

"Couldn't help yourself?" he started, the tapping accelerating.

Robert squirmed in his chair, trying to find a comfortable position that accommodated the handcuffs still around his wrists. There was no need to still wear them and Robert and Alex both knew it.

Alex leaned forward. "Claire wasn't enough?" he seethed.

Robert kept his face flat and said nothing. He kept his thoughts on Claire, still safely in the backyard, as far as he knew. They had been waiting for him but hadn't searched the house or yard. They didn't have enough for that. Yet.

"No lawyer?" Alex sighed, flipping through the paperwork on the table. He looked up with a shrug. "I guess you must be innocent, then." He couldn't help but smirk as he began to pull out document after document and neatly line them up against each other. A blurry photo still from security footage at Pachelbel's Lizard came next. Alex held it up beside his face and smiled.

"Robert, this was the first time I had any real physical link to you at a crime scene. You and that dirty old coat. But I was onto to you far, far before then," Alex stated. He set down the photo and tapped his temple. "I saw you."

Another photo was slammed down of an apartment complex.

"Fleming Towers," Alex said. "Christmastime. You killed Vincent Rove."

Robert stared at the photograph hard. He began to hear the sound of traffic in the annals of his memory. The glaring sting of car headlights reflecting in pools of rain. Robert's index finger began to twitch. Christmastime. *The racoon.*

Another photo.

"Elizabeth Monmouth," Alex stated. He bent down to interrupt Robert's frozen gaze. "On her way to get groceries for her grandmother, you prick."

*The deer.*

"That kid at Pachelbel's Lizard."

*The cricket.*

"Jacob Ponce."

*Piper.*

"You were getting too comfortable by Mercer Island."

*Grant's baby.*

Robert's hands were clenched in an attempt to keep the handcuffs from rattling. He was shaking deep inside, waves of memories crashing down on him before he had a chance to catch his breath. A key finally fit and unlocked the answer he was looking for. He was killing but he was bringing back life. One and then another. A balance between the living and dead. Claire had fit somewhere in the middle, in a void after Piper's raising but before the killing at Mercer Island. And now Grant's baby was back. Robert's mouth went dry. For Claire to come back, the scales would need to tip again.

"I need to make a phone call," Robert said suddenly. He pushed himself back from the table.

Alex tucked his hands into his pants pockets and rocked back and forth, relishing in Robert's accelerated breathing. He tried to calm his own racing heartbeat, thumping at the thought of all those doubting faces he could finally slap with the facts. And he thought of Claire Castle, almost at rest. "No problem," he said sourly, opening the door. "I'll arrange it."

---

Piper willed the phone to ring. *Ring.* She grew tired of carrying it in her hands, wandering all around the house from one end to the other, occasionally risking a look outside at the white tomb. Before he was taken away, Piper and Robert had agreed she would stay there, their exchanged looks telling each other why. But it had been too long. She heard nothing from Robert or of Robert on the news. It was just her, Claire's body, and Jasper, who sat in the dining room and stared intently through the glass door, fluctuating between low growls and high-pitched whines. Piper stood up from the couch, towering over Jasper's tense body as she followed his line of sight. There was a splatter of black within the white tent, an inky dark blot moving stealthily within the sacred place. Holding Jasper back, Piper squeezed through the glass door and quickly shut it behind her, igniting a rage of scratches.

Whipping back the folds of the white tent, Piper jumped at the sharp hiss that met her from the shadows. A black cat moaned and crawled forward, inching forward towards the thin sheet that discreetly covered Claire's still-lifeless body.

"Out!" Piper shouted, swatting at the animal.

The cat arched its back and hissed again, spittle dripping from its mouth. Both animal and human jerked at the sudden tone change in Jasper's incessant barks. Piper swatted at the cat one more time before running inside.

Robert stood at the kitchen counter, methodically rinsing, measuring, filling the coffee pot. He was still wearing the same clothes from the funeral, now dingier and creased with lines of sweat. He didn't look up until the coffee pot clicked and began the brewing cycle.

"I made bail," Robert explained, rubbing his face hard. "We need to talk." He looked through the window towards the white tent and back at Piper.

"No change," she said.

Robert sighed and filled a mug with the small amount of coffee brewed. He shuffled to the living room and sat down. Piper and Jasper followed him, both watching and waiting for Robert's next move. He looked at them, his mouth tight and grim. He thought he tasted death, like a lingering scratch at the back of his throat. His mind and soul had no recollection of killing but something in his body did. Something in him recognized the names Alex had shoved in his face. Something in him knew there had been more. Robert explained his revelation from his interrogation with Alex.

Piper was frozen in the center of the living room, listening. Her eyes flicked around the room, as though jumping from thought to thought. Maybe somewhere in her recognized, too. She finally returned her gaze to Robert. He was staring into his coffee, sinking down into its murky depths, wishing to be lost there forever.

"If this is true, why didn't Claire wake up after Mercer Island? Wouldn't that killing have brought her back to life before you could use it on Abby?" Piper could not believe what she was saying and that she was saying it in such a matter-of-fact tone."

"I don't know, I just don't know. Maybe I should have tried again with Claire? Started the process over? I don't know. How could I have known? Something isn't right. None of this is right." Robert shuffled his hair around violently as though trying to contain his jumbled thoughts.

"We need help," Piper stated suddenly, stomping her foot for emphasis.

Robert sat back and sighed, melting into the couch. "Piper..."

"No, really," she continued, holding up the phone. "And I know just who to call."

---

"Thank you for trusting the professionals at Our Nation's Psychic Network. You will be connected with your personal guide in just a few short moments."

The recorded message finished and the swanky hold music for Our Nation's Psychic Network continued over the speaker. Robert stared at the phone laying on the countertop, the bags under his eyes heavy with lack of sleep. Every breath he took looked more and more labored. Piper chewed her lip, hiding behind the walls of her coffee cup, willing this to work. Outside, the sun on yet another day was setting behind Claire's white tomb. Jasper laid at the glass sliding door, snarling quietly when his gaze locked with the dark creature inside. Everyone jumped when the hold music was interrupted by a velvety voice.

"Good evening," the voice whispered. "Who do I have on the line?"

Piper and Robert exchanged looks. Piper motioned for Robert to speak.

"Robert here," he said after clearing his throat. Even his vocal cords felt strained to ripping point.

"Robert," the voice repeated. Piper leaned forward, straining to hear. Either it was a bad connection or the psychic was trying to add to the performance. "Are you alone? I'm picking up on another presence."

Piper covered her mouth to silence her gasp. She shook her head at Robert.

"Uh, no," Robert said unconvincingly, trying to read Piper's hand motions. "Just me on the line."

"Right." The voice went flat. "What do you need help with, Robert?"

Robert stared at the phone, his face drooping. He hadn't thought this far out. He hadn't thought far out in a long time. He was living one breath to the next but struggling for each and every one of them. The light outside was almost gone. When morning came, he knew the day would end it all. Alex would return. He would connect him with another murder, they would realize what they had let loose. There would be no more bail. No more second chances. And that white tent would crumble beneath the elements and wash Claire away with it, forever spinning in a waterfall of light.

Robert stood up straight, gripping the countertop. *Forever spinning in a waterfall of light.*

Jasper's growls suddenly grew frantic as he leapt at the sliding door, scratching and biting at the glass. Piper went to the door to try to calm him down and met the eyes of the black cat, sitting complacently on the other side of the glass.

"Do you remember?" the voice whispered.

Robert closed his eyes and followed the darkness he found there. A faraway pinpoint of light called to him, a smell and a touch he had not felt in a long, long time.

Jasper howled and banged against the glass but the cat continued to stare inside, unflinching. Piper fell to her knees and grabbed the nearest wall as the house began to tremble.

"What's happening?" she shouted over Jasper's cries.

"Do you remember?" The voice on the phone was loud now, commanding.

Robert pressed his eyes shut so hard they ached. His hands convulsed against the countertop. He was getting closer and closer to the light, he felt the sweat gather across his body from the strain. A form began to take shape, limply spinning in the stream of light. It was a woman, he could tell by her cascading hair. He was almost there, almost within reach of the touch of her skin.

The house went completely dark and Piper screamed. The cat howled at them as the house began to rock back and forth.

Piper reached up and opened the sliding glass door, releasing Jasper on the feline outside. She tumbled forward as the ground pitched, causing splintering cracks in the cement patio. Jasper chased the cat into the white tent and Piper crawled after them. The two animals were at each other's throats, howling and tumbling across the loose soil around Claire's grave.

"Stop!" Piper shouted, searching around the tent for some sort of weapon, some way to separate the two creatures from each other. There was nothing, it was as pristine as a shrine. The ground continued to rumble and gurgle, as though boiling beneath the surface.

Finally, the animals broke apart and Jasper limped next to Piper. As she grabbed him and began to back out of the tent, the black cat rose onto its hind legs and hissed, spittle dripping from its razor teeth.

"Leave me!" the cat screeched.

Piper screamed and scrambled out of the tent, dragging Jasper with her. With a sudden drop, the ground settled and stopped shaking. She stumbled into the house and closed the door, locking it behind her. Jasper limped to hide beneath the dining room table, whining as quiet as a whisper.

Piper choked, fighting for words between her shallow breaths. She held her hands against the cold glass, watching for any kind of movement outside. The cat had talked. *The cat had talked.* Everything outside was now completely still. And as she turned to the kitchen, Robert was gone.

# CLAIRE

I loved Robert, I really did. Yes, I wanted a divorce. Yes, I planned to leave him. But that didn't change that I loved him, just in a different way. And he loved me. Even after he killed me.

We were too strangely alike, I think. Like mirrors reflecting each other, but the image was always skewed or just backwards. After we were married, I began to see my reflection was starting to transform, like a butterfly preparing to leave its cocoon. My miscarriages changed me and rightfully so. I formed and I deformed, I grew but then I would recede. But Robert never changed, never wavered. Even though I needed him to if we were ever going to fly off together. Even though I begged him to. Our house by the water became a house of a thousand tears, for me.

*The day of my death*. What a strange thing to say. We had fought up and down that entire week, over stupid things that we would walk away from but never pick up and resolve again. He knew what I was considering. I was never good at hiding things because I never wanted to. Took too much effort. He knew I was considering leaving him. Leaving us. Hairline fractures were appearing in our reflections. I think I just saw it earlier than Robert did.

What a horrible employee I was. I had too much time to myself unchecked. They should have never given me my own computer, I'm embarrassed to think of it now. I know the things they probably found. My obsessive personal checklists and pictures of cats. I had dozens of photos of various tropical locales so I could switch my desktop image every week and dream of those sandy beaches or snowy mountaintops or some field in between. And then there would be search histories about other jobs. About rooms for rent. About cheap divorce attorneys.

For all my big talk about leaving and breaking free, I have to admit I almost chickened out. So, I sent Robert a text, a commitment that I would be forced to follow up on later. That this weekend was the weekend. The one where I would really pack and leave and he'd be left with the clumps of dust I left behind. He could have the floating house, I'd take my chances. The next question was, when would I tell him? Outside my office or on our way home? It seemed wrong to sully those happy windows we'd pass in the long twilight. It seemed wrong to let our little world of unhappiness penetrate their own. Those thoughts are the last thing I am conscious of. And maybe that is a blessing.

Don't think it was all bad. I remember the nights. I remember the cold floors, huddled together in our sleeping bags, laughing into the dawn. I remember fingertips brushing against each other, electric highways that carried our spark like a trail of black powder. I remember blood, sweat, and tears. I remember his heavy breathing next to mine, the pounding of his heart reverberating up his chest cavity, over and over again until I fell asleep. Then I remember unraveling. I remember aching sadness, grieving the words that hung between us, waiting to be plucked and said, only to fade away forever. And just because I don't remember the grisly details, don't think it doesn't hurt. Robert took the final swing and now we are shattered, the dust of two reflections intermingled, together yet still an utter, useless waste.

The black cat? Yes, that was me. I am stuck in between, I am neither here or there. So I am allowed this as a way to wander before the darkness drives me mad. And when I found my body in my old backyard? Sorry Jasper and Coffee Shop Girl, I'm not going anywhere.

# THE SAD MAN

Caught midair in that dark place, Claire twirled slowly and limply in a never-ending loop, displayed like a trophy within a cascade of light, as though she was suspended underwater, forever snared beneath the choppy waves, the surface just within sight. She curved like this over and over, a celestial object orbiting a black star. Robert watched her, standing just on the light's edge. He studied her lines, the veins on her neck. Her closed eyelids twitched, as though fighting to open and tell the story of she and him and how it all ended. But she didn't need to tell him. In that dark place, Robert finally remembered.

His knees went out. He crumbled to the freezing cold floor, pressing his forehead into his clenched fists. Air was caught in his ribcage, he couldn't manage a full breath until he felt on the edge of blacking out. Glimpses of Claire's murder flooded his mind, strange moments that tied together the entire tale. He was the monster they all suspected. He was a walking, talking lie. He whispered into his horrible hands the question that always haunted him. *Why?*

"She wants to wake," Death announced. "But you have not won her back yet."

Robert looked up from the ground, his swollen eyes squinting at the pillar of light. Claire swirled above him like an electric cloud. He couldn't see the source of the voice but he could feel it, everywhere.

"You learned the balance. You learned it well," Death continued. "Do you understand what I require?"

Robert hung his head. Waves of nausea drowned him over and over again. The darkness closed in on him, he wanted to reach out and touch the light but feared the heat that emanated from it. Drawing himself into a sitting position, he finally spoke. "I can't," he whispered.

"Then she will sleep."

Robert looked up as Claire began to float higher and higher. He heard the cries of the people he had killed, even her own, in his throbbing ears. He began to crumble inside. He was worthless. A wife killer, he hurt the one person he swore to love and protect. He took one last look above before he would succumb to the darkness. *That should be me.*

Robert jerked suddenly. "What about me?" he cried out, struggling to his feet. He tried to reach up for Claire, but she was already becoming a flat shadow in the bright sky. "If you need another life, take me! Bring her back and take me!"

There was no response. All Robert could hear was his own heavy breathing. But Claire's ascension had ceased. Robert prayed harder than ever. He would leave it all behind. The floating house. Jasper. Piper. All of it.

"She died at your hand," Death said deeply. "It will require more than just your life. You will go back amongst the living as someone else and I will return your old body to the deep waters. But you will continue your service for me. Forever."

Claire's revolution in the sky paused, waiting for his answer. Her hair glistened in the light, just like it did after every morning shower. He remembered the warmth of her skin, pink and damp. Robert didn't need to say the words. If he could bring back that beautiful life, he would endure any consequence. As if in response, Claire's form began to descend. He reached up as she settled into his outstretched arms, just exactly how it had felt a thousand times before. Resting Claire on the ground, Robert cradled her in his arms. Her eyes were closed, soft and relaxed. He swept the hair out of her face and pressed his cheek to her forehead, soaking her scalp with his tears. Breathing her in for one last time. Why he had taken her beautiful life, he didn't know. He didn't need to know. He wasn't that man, anymore.

"If I could change it all," Robert whispered. "I would do anything."

# 1 DAY ALIVE

Piper knew she had nodded off to sleep several times. She couldn't help it, there was only so long she could stare at the thick black of the backyard before it all started to go fuzzy. She would awake with a start as her head thumped against the cold glass of the backdoor only to find Jasper snoring beside her. She and Jasper had spent the night planted on the dining room floor, door locked securely, jumping whenever the security light flickered due to some bat or passing bird. Piper kept the phone at her side, but it never rang. And the white tent remained still and quiet, with no sign of the talking black cat or Robert. It was her and Jasper against the night until finally the sun began to rise, casting a pink glow on the sleepy backyard.

All evidence of the evening earthquake was completely erased. There were no cracks in the patio, no signs of damage from the house rocking back and forth. No one ever called, no neighbor had come to see what the ruckus was about. It was as though it didn't happen. Or didn't happen to anyone else.

It was full on morning before Piper considered going outside. Two cups of very strong coffee and one long discussion with Jasper later, she finally unlocked the backdoor with a climatic crack. She almost tripped as Jasper rushed past her, diving into the white tent without hesitation. Piper paused, frozen, waiting for the howl and hiss of an altercation. But she heard nothing. Fearing the worst and imagining the cat had grown into some nightmarish behemoth overnight, Piper grabbed a nearby shovel and went charging into the tent.

---

Alex hadn't slept all night. He couldn't sleep, imagining how it would feel to know Robert Castle was finally, truly, completely caught. Their case was solid now. Robert had known it, too, Alex had seen it in his eyes. *Hope you enjoy your last night as a free man,* he thought as he prepared his clothes and paperwork for the next morning. At 3:00 am, Alex decided this was cause for celebration. He pulled out the worn and crinkled cigarette carton from his suit jacket and gingerly removed that final cigarette. His dark companion, still crisp and new as though it just packed. It was time to part ways for good. Lighting the cigarette, Alex watched each deep exhalation disappear into the thick night, evaporating neatly into nothing.

It was exactly 10:00 am when Alex knocked three times on the front door of Robert Castle's house. He smoothed his suit jacket, his heart pounding with caffeine, nerves, and lack of sleep. He had imagined this day for a long time. This was not just for himself but for Claire Castle. Glancing over his shoulder, Alex nodded at his backup gathered in their vehicles scattered across the street. He knocked again, firmly.

Alex jumped as a dog barked at him piercingly from the other side of the fence. He banged again on the front door, unlocking his gun holster. No answer. Car doors began to open behind him, Alex could hear the chatter of the police scanner scratch through the air. Sweat began to gather on his neck, beneath the thick folds of Alex's suit jacket. *Robert Castle was his to catch.* Trying the door, Alex found it locked. He approached the barking dog and scaled the fence, slipping as he landed on his shiny leather dress shoes. Jasper arched his back and danced around Alex, his body a mix of ruffled fur and wagging tail. Alex could hear the commotion behind him as the other officers gathered to follow his lead. He had to move fast.

Ignoring the little dog that tried to charge his feet, Alex rounded the corner and slipped into the empty backyard. It was a mess of dead plants, various yard tools, and a very large white tent. Peering into the house through the glass backdoor, Alex paused as he watched for any kind of movement. Nothing. Had Robert fled? Was he really that stupid? Alex's heart pumped harder and harder. His attention turned to the white tent as a high-pitched whistle rang out, causing the little dog to abruptly leave Alex and run into the tent.

"Found you," Alex whispered, his hands wrapped tightly around his gun as he approached the tent. The other officers had scaled the fence as well, he could hear their calls to each other as they cleared each corner. Charging towards the entrance, Alex whipped open the tent and pointed his gun nozzle inside.

Claire was sitting outside of her makeshift grave, propped up limply against Piper's shoulder. She was still in her burial clothes, a dress once featured in a dozen pictures and memories was now caked with black mud and insects. Her skin was strange and translucent, a pallid shade of gray. She looked up at Alex with heavy eyes and no sign of recognition, loose dirt crumbling from her stiff hair as she moved. Jasper nestled his head beneath her crumpled hand while keeping an eye on the man standing in the entrance.

Alex slowly holstered his gun. It was several moments later that he finally spoke. "Claire Castle?" He said her name in a whisper, as though it was too fragile to say any louder. He knelt to examine the face he had seen a thousand times displayed in crime scene photos, cold and lifeless. His eyes trailed to Piper, who was staring into the distance beyond the white tent. A commotion of voices in the backyard snapped back her attention.

"Get rid of them," Piper whispered harshly, motioning outside with one hand while the other remained firmly wrapped around Claire's bony torso.

Alex looked over his shoulder quickly then back again. "Where's Robert?"

"I don't know."

"Gone," Claire whispered hoarsely.

"Gone?" Piper repeated, looking down at Claire's face. She had struggled to look at it fully, to stare into the clouded eyes that had been shut for almost a year. She had pulled Claire from the ground like a rebirth of sorts, holding her there on the edge of the makeshift grave, waiting for Robert to appear.

Alex composed himself and slicked back his hair, turning to exit the tent and quickly shutting it closed behind him. Piper heard him ordering a search of the house and then everything became a blur. Once they were gone she would take Claire inside, who was already healing and knitting herself back together. Piper would care for her in all the ways that Robert had planned and prepped for, always believing that one day she would wake up and he would be ready for her. The details never mattered. As long as Claire returned, the job was done.

*Robert was gone.* Piper somehow knew it, too. She felt it. There was a part of him that was connected to her, the man that gave her a second chance, a new place in the cosmos. Piper looked down as Claire feebly squeezed her hand. She was going to need her. And Piper would need her, too.

# ROBERT

It was Alex that called her with the news. Claire recognized the number as it flashed across the screen. She, Alex, and Piper had stayed in close contact the last few months; Alex and Piper a bit more than they wanted to admit. They needed each other, they were comrades in a strange and unexplainable story. Alex took an impossible explanation and embraced it, maybe just to appease Piper or maybe because he'd seen enough of Robert to believe it. She wondered how he had her number stored in his phone, because Claire wasn't Claire Castle, anymore. That Claire was still dead. She had assumed a new name, yet another rebirth in her continuing saga. But memories of the old Claire still lingered, captured in photos and the coffeemaker and even Jasper himself. She couldn't discard all of the past.

When she picked up the phone, Claire knew the reason for the call. That last part of Robert still remained out there somewhere, the part that once housed his soul. It was autumn now and the leaves that lined the streets of Seattle matched her bright orange coat as she weaved quickly through the meandering pedestrians. When she arrived at Robert's old workplace at the Port of Seattle, her throat tightened at the police presence. This was really happening. Locating Robert's missing body was the last piece she needed before she could finally leave Claire Castle behind.

In the mix of uniformed and suited officers, Claire picked out Alex's shiny hair. He knew she'd be there, she told him she'd race to catch this moment. He was standing next to the stretcher, his hand firmly planted there. He had finally found Robert and he wasn't letting go just yet.

"Look at me," Claire whispered, barely breathing as she gripped the railing of the pier.

Finally, Alex looked up and scanned the curious crowd gathered there. He spotted Claire's orange coat, locking eyes with her and nodding. *It was him.* She didn't have to see Robert, or what was left of him. Over a year beneath the water was not going to leave much. But just to see the black bag and the outline of something real and tangible laying within it was enough.

As she watched Robert's body disappear into the waiting van, Claire Castle was finally gone. And for her, that dark version of Robert was gone, too. He had died the same day as her, Claire just never knew how or where. He had taken his own life, arriving at Death's doorstep not long after her. She chose to remember that Robert. The one that struck a bargain for her return, the part of the story where she comes back and starts again.

# ABOUT THE AUTHOR

Erin Ritch founded her indie press No Wyverns Publishing in 2015. In addition to her three novels and short story collection, Erin's work has also appeared on The Manifest Station. She lives in rural Oregon with her husband, two daughters, and an Irish Terrier named Arthur Pendragon.

Follow Erin:
Websites: ErinRitch.com & NoWyverns.com
Facebook.com/ErinRitchAuthor
Twitter: @Eritch324
Instagram: @nowyvernspublishing

# ABOUT THE ILLUSTRATOR

Char Houweling is a professional graphic designer and freelance illustrator. She enjoys drawing, playing video games, riding her bike, and more drawing.

You can view more of her work at:
Website: HouwelingDesign.com
Facebook.com/houwelingart

# AVAILABLE FROM ERIN RITCH

Myth
Memories Wait Alone
The Quinn Family Adventures: The Mayan Ruins
No Wyverns Publishing Short Story Collection: Volume One

Made in the USA
Middletown, DE
15 November 2021

52107118R00071